AN INVITATION
TO DEATH

AN INVITATION
TO DEATH

Anil Thakraney

Srishti
PUBLISHERS & DISTRIBUTORS

SRISHTI PUBLISHERS & DISTRIBUTORS
Registered Office: N-16, C.R. Park
New Delhi – 110 019
Corporate Office: 212A, Peacock Lane
Shahpur Jat, New Delhi – 110 049
editorial@srishtipublishers.com

First published by
Srishti Publishers & Distributors in 2015

To Kanchan and Bedoli.

Thanks to Vasudha Narayanan
for the cover design, and special thanks to
Ralph Rebello for his valuable inputs.

Imogen was on deputation to help with the launch of a British lifestyle magazine's Indian edition. She had tired of the few boring men she had dated in Mumbai. The routine had sickened her; the coffee invitation, the red roses, the movies, the making-out, and the frantic demand for sex. It was like Indian men were being produced in a moron factory. Imogen had been warned about the average Indian male's attitude to western women: A white chick is equal to an easy lay. That was the reason why her eyes lit up when she first met Darius at the Jehangir Art Gallery.

This guy was real fun. He was intelligent, and he did the unexpected. He would gaze into her eyes and discuss the global economic crisis, and effortlessly find humour in such a dry topic. Darius was crazy, magnetic crazy. But what turned her on the most was his spontaneity. That day, as they sat hand in hand by the sea at Cuffe Parade's 'Lover's Point', a tiny little spot which the 'moral police' had not discovered as yet, in the midst of a philosophical discussion on life and death, Darius put out a tantalising offer.

"Babes, let's do Goa."

Imogen was taken aback, even though she had wanted to go there ever since she had set foot on Indian soil. She hadn't been able to do so, because the Indian designers were taking their own sweet time to comprehend the magazine's international template. An instant 'yes' would mean she was an easy lay, and she didn't want Darius to assume that. Not so soon, at least.

"Yeah sure, good idea."

"Great. There's a bus that leaves in two hours from Bandra. I have a pal in Goa whose pad we can use. He and his wife won't mind; they'll love having us over."

"Whoa! Just like that? You must be kidding!"

"I'm serious, it will be fun. Screw the clothes; we'll get you some cool stuff at the flea market. And don't worry about the magazine… the locals perform only when put under pressure." He grinned.

Imogen was stunned, but the thought of travelling to Goa without a plan with this oh-so-cool man was too good to resist. Indeed, it was the man's insanity that had attracted her to Darius in the first place. Fearing that hesitation would kill the moment, all she could blurt out was, "Fuck it, let's go."

SUSHANT SINGH WAS EMPLOYED WITH THE DELHI CRIME branch. Usually an affable man, three things sent his blood pressure shooting up. Phone calls from pesky politicians, constant nagging by his always-suspicious missus, and the rape and murder of city girls. Because all three happened regularly in his life, Singh was constantly on the edge. Not a nice man to know.

It had been a particularly nasty day. A rather impolite text message had arrived from the boss about an unsolved case. It had been three months since the mutilated corpse of a young Vasant Kunj housewife had been discovered in a shady hotel room. Naina Mehra's beautiful body had been so badly ravaged, that even the otherwise indifferent forensics chap had puked all over the crime scene. The limbs had been severed from the body, the head smashed with what must have been a heavy object, and most gruesome of all, a large screwdriver had been shoved into her genitals. And there were traces of dried semen on the victim's face. Technically not rape, but close.

The police had immediately suspected her husband, a marketing manager, but it was later found he had been travelling at the time. The investigation had gone nowhere, much like the infamous Aarushi Talwar murder mystery, and the case had been transferred to the crime branch. The officers had unearthed zilch so far; they had failed to arrive at a single suspect despite a 360-degree investigation.

Singh was seething with rage; he didn't like to fail. He summoned his deputy. "Let's start from scratch. This bloody Naina has screwed my happiness."

GLORIA GOMES AND HER HUSBAND RAN A LITTLE RESORT OFF Baga beach. A very basic setup. You had to run around to get hold of a bucket of warm water for a bath, and mosquito bites were the only complimentary item on the scanty menu. But the Gomes were usually full-up. The reason for their success, as some of the male visitors privately explained: At seven each morning, Gloria would emerge from her cottage for a swim. And that shapely body in a two-piece black bikini made the visitors forget all about the blood-thirsty insects. Gloria was, of course, aware of the prying eyes. But she didn't mind. In fact, she looked forward to the morning ritual. It had been some years since Joaquin Gomes had looked at her in that way. Lust does see a downward spiral in every relationship, even in a romantic place like Goa.

However, that morning, things weren't looking so rosy. The couple that had checked in two days ago had still to make the advance payment, and the room door hadn't been opened yet. The service boy, the only one the cost-cutting Gomes had cared to hire, felt something was amiss. After a great deal of hesitation, mainly because of the cost of installing a new lock as they had lost the spare key, the muscular Joaquin rammed the door open.

The resort was never the same again. And the owner was never spotted again in a two-piece black bikini at seven in the morning.

THE NATIONAL AND INTERNATIONAL MEDIA WENT BERSERK. A young English magazine designer had been found slaughtered in the room of a hip Goa resort. This was a sensational story and it had the news television journalists salivating.

"We can play this one for days," smiled the portly anchor, famous for going ballistic over juvenile stories.

And this one was big, really big. It was global. There had already been much talk over the lack of safety of foreign women in India, and what made the incident even more horrifying was the numbing similarity with the Vasant Kunj housewife murder three months ago, with the identical mutilation and dried semen on the victim's lips. Only this time, instead of a screwdriver, it was a torch. A biggish Eveready torch. This slaughter was going to feed many mouths in the Indian media. Owners and CEOs of television networks got into the act and called for urgent brainstorming sessions on how the story could be used to maximise advertising revenues.

JEROO IRANI WAS AN ANGST-RIDDEN OLD LADY. SHE HAD BEEN convinced for many years that life had dealt her a really bad card. She had lost her boozer of a husband to liver cirrhosis at a young age, leaving her alone to raise their only son. The savings were meagre and private tuitions to academically-challenged kids from down-market Colaba schools didn't bring in much income. And even that source had dried up some years ago, as the parents no longer believed the lady was sane. The constant battle for survival had turned Jeroo into a cranky aunty, the sort of neighbour you desperately try to avoid encountering in the elevator. And yet, twenty years ago, there had been one thing that had brought a glimmer of hope to her forever gloomy eyes. Darius had turned out to be a bright student at school, intelligent way beyond his age. By the ninth standard, when other kids were busy with adventures of Tintin and the Hardy Boys, he had already devoured Shakespeare, Hawking and Tagore, and could hold forth on any subject. The mediocre school teachers were obviously intimidated by this lad, and would ensure he got high grades so that they wouldn't have to deal with him. Even the Marathi teacher, the one subject Darius regularly flunked, would do the same. Yes, Jeroo had a reason to smile, but it vanished from her face soon after her son turned eighteen. Things went horribly wrong thereafter.

MUMBAI'S CRIME BRANCH OFFICE AT CRAWFORD MARKET WAS buzzing with activity. A young city-based British girl had been killed in Goa, and the state Home Minister was very keen that the case be dealt with as a high priority one. He had no faith in Goa cops. The British High Commission had already spoken to the Minister to try and get to the bottom of the matter as soon as possible. The women's rights ladies had been haranguing the Minister even at lunch hour, and something had to be done quickly. Goa's Chief Minister was on the edge as well. Goa's main source of revenue has always been international tourists, and therefore he didn't like this mess at all. The media circus was already on; each evening, puerile discussions had gotten underway on the lack of safety measures for women. TV dinner debates in India are more gas than substance, but they do help to energise the usually lazy politicians. In this case, the pressure on politicians had been quickly palmed off to the crime branch officers.

A team was swiftly dispatched to Goa. ACP Rakesh Kamble was named the team leader. Kamble loved solving crimes of passion; he had his own sexual fetishes, and this particular murder had got him very excited. Another delicious factor was the similarity with the crime committed in Delhi, and if there's one thing crime branch sleuths in Mumbai like more than solving crimes, it's the chance to outwit their Delhi counterparts. And that sentiment is mutual.

AZEEM KHAN BEAMED AS HE SAT ON THE PORCH OF HIS Coonoor bungalow, sipping mint tea and watching sunlight bathe his modest apple farm. This was the life he had always dreamed of, back in the days when he was chasing criminals in Bombay. A dream he never imagined would come true. And that's because Khan had a problem with his DNA. It carried that rare Indian gene called 'honesty', and that meant the cop was always low on funds. What had helped was that his wife Zeenat had inherited some wealth from her father, and once she offered to pitch in, the Coonoor bungalow became a reality.

Zeenat arrived, a mug of filter coffee in hand (the two differed on taste in their choice of brew, among other things), and ruffled Khan's all-gray hair as she sat down beside him. She felt very happy for her man; he deserved this luxurious retirement after a hard life, most of which was spent crawling through Bombay's underbelly. And she felt happy for herself too. The tranquility had been hard won; all those nights spent worrying about whether her husband would return home the next morning. And she'd never forget Khan's encounter with Sainath, the dreaded serial killer. How could she ever. Khan, as if reading her thoughts, pulled her close. Winter had set in and it was cold in Coonoor despite the bright sunlight. Together, sipping different drinks, they stared fondly at their private garden.

"Tonight I shall make some apple milkshake for Khan; he'll like that. And the apples will come from our own farm." Zeenat had swiftly moved her mind to more pleasant things. Sainath must be confined to the dustbin. He must.

THE SCENE AT THE GOMES MOSQUITO RESORT WAS CHAOTIC. Goa cops had swung into action, and were doing their best to keep the Mumbai crime branch officers in check. And, to add to their frustration, the Delhi sleuths had descended too, having heard about the similarity of the crime with the unsolved one in their own backyard. It was a turf war – a war that the much-harried Gloria could have done without. She politely asked them to get on with their investigation, and then leave her alone. Meanwhile, the post mortem report was out:

Death due to head injury, and dismemberment of body post death. Semen was found absent in the private parts, indicating there had been no penile penetration. A torch had been inserted with force into the victim's genitals. Identity of the victim had been established through her passport. Imogen Parsons. Aged 25. British national.

Gloria reported that the couple had arrived unannounced early in the morning two days ago, and had pleaded for a room. As luck would have it, a Danish gay couple had checked out at noon, and so, yes, she provided them space. They were checked-in using Imogen's passport as proof of identity. The Mumbai and Delhi cops were appalled to find that no questions had been asked about the couple's relationship and were rather annoyed when told that in Goa, no one asked such stupid questions.

But the bigger problem was that Gloria, her husband and the room service boy could only provide a vague description of the male companion. Tall, perhaps six feet, and well built. He was wearing a blue t-shirt, jeans, a baseball cap and dark glares, which meant the description would not be of much help to the sketch artist. He was also carrying a stuffed rucksack. Rakesh Kamble quickly figured he was in trouble. He threw a knowing glance at Sushant Singh, who had joined him inside the resort's tiny office, a storeroom that had been sexed up. Both the officers, usually cold towards each other, realised this was a dead end.

"But a lot of leg work for Kamble in Mumbai," Singh smiled to himself. And he headed off to the closest beach shack for some booze and bird-watching.

KAMBLE WALKED INTO THE WOMEN'S HOSTEL WITH A SPRING in his stride. Being surrounded by a bevy of beauties wasn't a regular occurrence in his life; he usually dealt with terrorists and rapists. Kamble glad-eyed a buxom woman, perhaps in her early thirties. As he waited for one Geeta Kulkarni to arrive at the reception area, the cop imagined Miss Buxom giving him a blow job at Baga beach. A nervous voice shattered the day-dream. "Sir, you asked for me? What can I do for you?"

Geeta, the hostel warden had informed him, was Imogen's roommate and friend. She worked for an advertising agency as an art director. Kamble came straight to the point, almost rudely, his fantasy blow job having been interrupted.

"How long did you know this girl Imogen Parsons?" He pronounced the name as 'Emojan Prasoon'.

Geeta had feared this shit would arrive at her doorstep to smear her face, and it had. "Around one year, sir."

"When did you last meet her?"

"Last week, sir. She called to say she was travelling for a few days for work. She hurriedly said something about a photo shoot for her magazine, and I didn't ask anything more."

"Did she have a boyfriend?"

"I don't know, sir. We never discussed such things."

"That's hard to believe. Two girls who are good friends, sharing the same room, and not discussing men?" Kamble asked sarcastically.

"Really, sir. She never told me anything about the men in her life. *Aai shappath!*" Geeta exclaimed in Marathi for effect as it always worked with the traffic cops. But it seemed to have no effect on this offensive man.

Watching her sweat and sniffle, Kamble's bushy eyebrows darted up. But he quickly dismissed the observation, assuming it could be the poor girl's first encounter with a policeman. He left Geeta weeping, who then rushed to her room. She collapsed on the bed she used to share with Imogen, and continued sobbing.

NAINA AND SUJIT HAD BEEN MARRIED FOR ONLY A YEAR, AND yet, as they dined at Punjabi by Nature at Saket's buzzing mall, a stranger would have assumed they had been together for the longest of times. They appeared pretty bored of each other, and were mechanically digging into the Galouti kebabs. It had been an arranged marriage, which is quite common in Delhi, and Naina's family had to arrange for a hefty dowry, also quite common in Delhi. She was a trained microbiologist and was keen to work after marriage, but Sujit would have none of it. As soon as the honeymoon in Mauritius was over (there wasn't an opening in her body that her partner hadn't crudely tried to penetrate), she had hesitatingly broached the issue one morning.

Sujit was no longer the suave, sophisticated charmer she had met for lunch at Maurya's Bukhara restaurant, their first 'private' meeting, arranged by the two families. He had revealed his true colours on the first night of their marriage, so the response hadn't really shocked Naina.

"Forget about it, I don't need your piddly salary. I don't want to come home to a wife who's tasted shit and piss all day. I want to return to a sexy woman who's geared up for action."

Without even waiting for her response, Sujit had smiled and zipped off to work in the milky white Skoda Laura, which had been a 'gift' from Naina's 'large-hearted' dad.

"How come you aren't getting pregnant, what's the bloody problem?" Sujit broke the pregnant silence while gesturing to the waiter to refill his plate. Naina kept quiet; she knew it was in her interest to not answer this question. Any response would ensure a few blows on the face later at night, accompanied by the choicest Punjabi cuss words. It might even happen right there at the restaurant.

Dejected with life, and reluctant to share her domestic strife with her parents (she knew they'd show no empathy), Naina would spend her day emptily browsing Khan Market's bookshops. One noon, something unexpected happened at Bahrisons. A tall, good-looking man tapped her on the shoulder.

"Hey, have you read Dalrymple's latest book, *Return of a King*? If not, I have a hunch you'll really like it. Allow me to buy you a copy, and don't say no. I like to gift books; they are my only passion."

Naina, although taken aback, smiled widely. For the first time in her life after her marriage, a complete stranger had spoken to her, and she had long forgotten how it felt to receive a gift.

"Hi, no. I'll pick it up myself, thanks," was all she could manage. The stranger was persistent, warmly persistent.

"Hey, no sweat, it's cool, really. Let's make a deal. I get you Dalrymple, you get me coffee and cookies. Okay?"

The man's magnetic smile was hard to resist, and so was the tempting offer.

Naina had met Darius. And the meeting had changed her life.

JEROO WOKE UP LATE THAT MORNING, FOR IT HAD BEEN A terrible night. Arthritic pain had kept her up till late, and she could not muster enough strength to reach for the painkillers she stored in her little medicine box, which she placed on top of her ancient, dysfunctional Godrej refrigerator. Grumpy, she managed to get herself off the bed, and amble towards the kitchen to make some tea. She had switched to black to cut costs on milk; just one of the many cuts she had enforced in her daily expenditure in order to survive. In the kitchen, she was greeted by a slithering snake. Jeroo shrieked, and momentarily forgetting the arthritis, scampered towards the living room where five more snakes wished her good morning. Darius was sprawled on the floor, and on the dusty old three-seater rexine sofa, she spotted a snoring stranger.

Jeroo kicked Darius on his back. "What the hell is this fellow doing here? Did he bring the snakes? Get up, you bloody swine."

Darius opened one eye, yawned loudly, and burst into hysterical laughter. "Mom, aren't these cuties so cool? Can I keep one in the house?" He darted towards one resting in a corner, lifted it up and started fondling it, almost erotically. Meanwhile the rudely awoken snake charmer was already up, and he rushed to get his pets back into the basket.

Ignoring her son's request, Jeroo caught the snake charmer by the collar and punched him on the nose.

"Get out of my house, you bastard, before I get you arrested!"

The charmer, still to gather his wits, hurriedly picked up the basket and rushed out. Darius dropped onto the sofa, and continued to laugh. The more his mother got agitated, the more the son enjoyed it.

"Relax mommy, they weren't poisonous, and they were so goddamned pretty."

Muttering cuss words, Jeroo headed towards the toilet, the only one in the house. She had given up on her son a long time ago. He would disappear for days together and she had gotten used to this lifestyle. And Darius would often bring his shady pals to sleep over. He had once picked up a volatile eunuch from the streets. But the snake charmer was a new low. Jeroo shuddered, thinking about what awaited her next, as she squeezed a little Colgate on her toothbrush that had seen better days. The Colgate family tube lasted for a year in the Irani household.

Of course, Jeroo had no idea Darius had arrived from Goa late at night. And had invited his co-passenger in the bus to stay over. What her son had been up to, Jeroo didn't know, and she didn't even care.

IMOGEN HAD LOST FAITH IN RELATIONSHIPS. HAVING GROWN up watching her now divorced parents try to claw each other's eyes out every other day, and then dump their frustrations on her, she would scoff when her pals brought up the subject of marriage and commitment. Laughing out loud on the subject provided a degree of healing to the emotional scars collected over the years. The young designer had begun experimenting with booze and drugs from her school days in London, but she had kept those habits private in Mumbai, not sure how her judgemental Indian colleagues would react.

The problem wasn't that she was averse to having short-term affairs in Mumbai; Imogen hadn't met anyone who interested her. The guys repulsed her on the very first date. She looked for madness in her man, and that could have been a desire born out of watching a perfectly happy marriage between two sane individuals degenerate into a farce. This cynical girl wanted to date a wacko, and she found one in Darius. Not just that, Darius Irani was entertainment in high-definition with surround sound.

It was a chance encounter at the art gallery. With nothing better to do on a Saturday afternoon, Imogen was trying hard to appreciate the mediocre artworks on display. Darius crept up from behind, and immediately started an evaluation of the painting for her benefit, without caring to introduce himself.

"Hey, you must watch that landscape carefully; there's a hidden mystery in it."

Imogen turned around and glared at the man. She was annoyed with the intrusion, but decided to go along. He looked okay.

"That's not the setting sun, it's the face of a demon peering over the hills to express rage about the way planet earth is going about things. I'm not joking, look closely."

Amused, Imogen decided to indulge the stranger. She bent over for a closer look, but found no demons. She smiled nonetheless. Encouraged, Darius pressed further, not bothering to lower his voice.

"On second thoughts, it's a fat-faced pervert desperately trying to hump the hills." And he broke out into a laugh. Along with them, there was an old lady and a middle-aged couple inside the gallery. The three, not wanting to be noticed, quietly slunk out of the room. Imogen smiled widely this time, pleased to meet someone who also found the paintings to be a sham. Darius then came up with something even more unexpected.

"Lady, you have two bucks to spare? I need to use the loo. Fuckers charge money out here for what should be a basic human right."

Happy to help, Imogen reached for her wallet, and found a fifty-rupee note as the lowest denomination. Darius didn't bother to wait; he grabbed it from her hand.

"Cool! Wait for me outside the men's room. I'll return the forty-eight bucks."

He didn't wait for a response. Smiling, he rushed out of the room, happily aware that this chick was nailed. Darius knew how to spot the right ones, and then use them for food and fun. Of course, she accepted the beer invite to Café Mondegar. Of course, she dated him, and of course, there was a lot of making-out. That's how it always panned out with Darius. He knew the routine only too well.

Imogen flew high with the man in more ways than one. This was the sort of man she always wanted to have a fling with, and now she had found him. She knew it wouldn't last long; it was apparent this crazy chap would tire of her sooner or later, and Imogen was fine with that arrangement. The stint in India would end soon, and she'd have to return home to London. Imogen wanted the fun to last as long as possible.

SUSHANT SINGH WAS BACK IN DELHI, HIS GOA SOJOURN A failure, though ogling at the voluptuous Russian swimmers had been fun. He dreaded having to share that with the chief of Delhi's crime branch, so he began thinking all over again. "Get back to the basics, Sushantji; someone must have spotted the killer with Naina."

Her neighbour, another Punjabi housewife (she preferred to call herself 'lady of leisure'), had earlier informed the cops that Naina had told her she would sometimes visit Khan Market in the afternoons to kill time, but the neighbour wasn't sure if Naina had been speaking the truth. Clearly, the lady had been influenced by all the tabloid gossip over dead Naina's 'loose character', but the police had taken her information seriously. Checks had been made at the various coffee shops, book stores and other retail outlets, but nobody had reported having seen Naina.

Singh summoned two of his trusted deputies, and they decided to scour Khan Market all over again. In any case, he had to seem busy in front of his colleagues after the time wasted in Goa. This time, the enquiry was carried out on a grand scale, with the victim's picture shown to every single staffer at every single retail outlet and restaurant. And this time the team got lucky. Bahrisons' store manager, who had been on sick leave during the earlier search operation, hesitatingly recognised Naina. She would visit now and then to browse, and would occasionally seek his advice on a title she had found interesting. When asked why he hadn't come forward with the information on his own, the chap said he wasn't really sure. Singh felt a strong urge to deliver a stinging slap, but was too excited with the sudden break. However, the excitement was short-lived as the man could not recollect seeing anyone accompany Naina at any time.

"Sir, she was always alone, and she always had a sad expression on her face. Poor woman."

Another dead end.

DARIUS HAD NO PLANS TO VISIT DELHI, BUT HE HAD TO TRAVEL to escape the cops who were looking for him. It was a harmless pub brawl, to Darius's mind, and he even joked about it with fellow passengers on the Rajdhani Express. But the proprietor of the beer bar located near Metro cinema hadn't found the incident amusing. Darius had downed six large beers and was trying to sneak out through the rear exit when an alert waiter spotted him. A hot chase ensued all the way to CST station, but by that time, Darius had managed to give his pursuer the slip. Not only was he an athletic man, Darius was familiar with every nook and cranny of the area, having spent many nights walking, doping and crashing on the streets.

But Darius being Darius, he wasn't going to let this interesting episode die down just like that. A few days later, he arrived at the bar's closing hour and waited in a dark corner for the man who had ratted on him. He then stalked the waiter and followed him all the way to his home at Saat Rasta, off Mahalakshmi Station. Darius barged into the *kholi* right in front of his wife and two little children, and rained heavy blows on the rat's face. Before the stunned victim could react, Darius was gone.

The proprietor of the bar, accompanied by the injured waiter, filed a police complaint the following day, and the assaulter's sketch was drawn. Usually cops in Mumbai don't pay attention to such trivial matters, but Prakash Shetty, the bar owner, had 'connections' with the local police. Darius had got tipped off by a police informer that the cops were looking for him. In this case, the informer's allegiance lay with the culprit, because Darius would often sell him hash at a discounted rate.

Darius did what he knew best – ransack mom's cupboard while she was away buying groceries at the Colaba market ration shop. He then boarded a BEST bus to Mumbai Central station. The next train departing was the Rajdhani. He didn't bother to purchase a ticket, and casually walked into a bogie. He enjoyed giving ticket collectors a hard time.

Inside an upper middle class home at Vasant Kunj, a young housewife had no idea a beer bar tiff miles away was about to prove costly for her.

RAKESH KAMBLE'S EFFORTS HAD ALSO BEEN IN VAIN. THE description provided by Mrs. Gomes was of no help, and the dead girl's hostel mate seemed to know nothing. His team conducted enquiries in the magazine office where Imogen worked, but her colleagues were clueless. In fact, they were surprised to hear she was dating someone. Each one of her male colleagues had tried to hit on her, and had failed miserably. A few of them appeared not very sad to hear of Imogen's gruesome end, but years of police work told Kamble they weren't suspects, just jealous guys happy that the snooty Brit had got her comeuppance.

And Imogen's phone calls had indicated nothing. Most of the calls were made to her friends in London, or were work-related. A random check was done on the contacts she called most often, and their call records indicated none of them was in Goa at the time of the murder. Her conversations on Facebook didn't throw up anything either; there was no talk of travel to Goa, there weren't any romantic chats either. The dead girl was quite inactive in the virtual world. Constables who had been instructed to look for leads at railways stations, bus stands and the airport had come up with nothing so far.

Kamble realised he was up against a wall. This was the handiwork of a really smart mystery man who had left absolutely no footprints. It was possible Imogen had checked into the Goa resort with a bum she picked up from the beach. This thought crossed Kamble's mind, and it made his conservative (when it came to 'family women') mind very uncomfortable. He wanted to rule out the possibility, and yet was aware it was a distinct option. A white girl, after all, is an easy lay, he reminded himself.

"Perhaps another trip to Goa is called for. And Delhi too. Need to check if the crime branch there has managed to unearth anything on the Naina Mehra murder case."

Despite his allergy to policemen from India's capital city, Kamble was gradually coming round to a hurtful reality: This case seemed beyond his capabilities. He needed help, and urgently too.

NAINA WAS DEEPLY FASCINATED WITH THIS MAD MAN. SHE HAD never met anyone like him. Darius would talk incessantly, flirt outrageously, and he made her feel beautiful once again. Although the boys in Kirori Mal College would routinely lust after her, Naina had stopped feeling beautiful after her marriage. Sujit treated her purely as a sex object. He showed no interest after the sex was over. It was like he was humping a life-size doll with big plastic tits.

Darius made her feel happy and desirable. He was funny, effervescent, well-read and sensitive. When the waiter at the coffee shop 'accidently' touched her shoulder, Darius gave the creep a stinging mouthful. Naina really liked that. Sujit, on the other hand, would have quickly looked the other way, or checked his Facebook page for new pictures posted by his female 'friends'. Naina was disappointed to learn that Darius was in Delhi on assignment as a photographer, and that he would be in the city for just a few days. He'd have to get back home to Mumbai after that. Which is why, when he invited her to his hotel room, she found it hard to decline.

"Naina, you must come over to my room. I want to show you some lovely pictures I recently shot."

"Hmm, I would really like that. But I might be busy tomorrow; we have guests coming over."

"Aww, come on! You can always steal an hour for yourself. I will shoot some cool pictures of you. You'll love them, I promise."

"I am not sure, it's difficult..."

"Listen, truth is, we may never meet again. Don't think too much, come over tomorrow any time. It will be fun." He quickly scribbled the hotel name and address on a tissue paper, folded it neatly and slipped it into her hand. And then gently kissed her hand.

Darius was a persuasive man, very hard to turn down. And Naina didn't want to turn him down, but was nervous about meeting a stranger in a hotel room. A stranger she felt attracted to. Later that evening when she read the note in the toilet, she discovered it was a hotel located close to the New Delhi railway station. Naina had never heard of the place. She suspected it would be a shady joint, and this discouraged her. But the thought of another night with Sujit helped make up her mind.

"I'll go. Don't want to miss out on this, and no one will find out anyway. If Sujit can blatantly cheat on me, there's no harm if I make a new male friend."

AZEEM KHAN RELUCTANTLY SCANNED THE NEWSPAPERS IN the Coonoor Club reading room to kill time. His friend and club member, retired Admiral Mahinder Khanna, was running late as usual for their weekly whisky meet. Khan had snapped all contact with the media ever since he had moved to the hill station. He saw no point in keeping in touch with the world down there. The news depressed him, and most of the stories involved crime and corruption. He had moved on from 'all that crap', as he termed it.

However, a report on the front page of one daily, which carried details of two murders that were similar in nature, caught his attention. Unable to look away, he read the story, and years of chasing criminals told Khan this was the work of a serial killer. Memories of Sainath flashed in his head, and he dropped the newspaper. "It was a bad idea reading this rubbish. I should have gone to the lawn for a stroll."

Thankfully, his pal arrived just then, and after a few large pegs of Vat 69, the twin murders faded very quickly from his memory.

DARIUS WAS CHILLING WITH HIS DOPE GANG IN A SECLUDED spot off Horniman Circle. The item usually on the menu was hash, but if one of the guys managed to sneak in a little cocaine, it was party time. This was a regular *adda* for the group of four. Horniman Circle is a business district that gets desolate after eight in the evening. And the local cops usually ignore the place. It makes sense to patrol happening areas. They are also wary of apprehending drug addicts as a few have the habit of attacking nosey *havaldars* with syringes loaded with the AIDS virus.

Darius would not be asked to dutch in for the smokes, for he contributed to the group with entertainment. Unlike Darius, his pals had regular jobs, so they didn't mind him parasiting. When you are stoned, a berserk man belting out stunning insights on the Milky Way can be a lot of fun.

However, tonight the usually boisterous man was subdued. The rest didn't know what was bothering him and they didn't even care, because they were sure the volcano would erupt at any moment. They had no idea Darius's mind was buzzing with dangerous thoughts. After years of indulging in petty crimes, he seemed to have found his calling. The two murders had been hugely delightful. He had tasted blood. Darius took in deeper drags from the joint, passed it around, and smiled to himself. This had been as easy as punching that asshole waiter, and a lot more fun. He'd like to do it again, and he'd like to try out a new city. The more number of cops chasing him, the greater the high. Savio laughed loudly as he looked at the silent Darius smiling to himself.

"Dude, you are in love!"

At last he spoke. "Yes man, I sure am."

That night, a famished Darius reached home earlier than usual. Agitated, Jeroo pounced on him, demanding to know if he had been stealing, as things were missing from her cupboard. The son didn't bother to respond; he headed to the kitchen, yanked open a few containers, hoping to find something to munch. Finding them empty, he shouted a few cuss words and proceeded to lie down on the sofa.

But Jeroo was adamant. She followed him, repeating the query louder this time. With the speed of a leopard that's cornered, Darius leaped towards her and punched her on the chest. "Fuck off, mom, leave me alone."

She went tumbling down to the ground. After a few minutes, heaving with pain, Jeroo managed to crawl to the bedroom. As she slid into the bed, the elderly lady cursed the gods. And her dead husband for leaving her alone with a loser.

NAINA'S END CAME WITHOUT MUCH PAIN. SHE WAS IN BED with Darius at a dodgy hotel, close to the bustling railway station. With a great deal of noise all around, her muffled cries could not have been heard by anyone. Darius had jumped on her as soon as she walked into the trap. This was not the sensitive, charming man Naina had coffee with the previous day, and past experience with that chameleon Sujit told Naina she was in trouble…big trouble. But with the strong arms clasped tightly around her large breasts, she realised it was too late to walk away. Instead, Naina tried to talk him out of it.

"Er, why don't we go to a restaurant around here and look at your pictures?" She turned around to make eye contact, and managed a faint smile. Darius's response was hysterical laughter.

"Relax ma'am, all that will happen in good time. I first need to examine all the goodies on your body."

He forced Naina onto the bed. She tried to get away, but it was no use. The thought of screaming occurred to her, but as a cheating housewife, she knew that wouldn't be a very good idea. Darius stripped off her purple and yellow *salwar kameez* in a matter of seconds, and then yanked off the black bra, as one would a wrapper from an inviting chocolate bar. Naina let out a faint scream, and this led to a hard punch on her face. She made no noise after that, hoping the rape would be swift. Off came the panties. Naina shut her eyes.

After that, Naina had no idea what was happening. Darius smashed her head with a large object. Death was instantaneous. The attacker then severed her limbs with a sharp knife, which Darius always carried on his person, just in case the street gangs turned on him. And then he turned himself on and sprayed dead Naina's face with his semen.

Task accomplished, it was time to say good-bye. Darius wore the cheap blonde wig he had flicked from Chor Bazaar back in his school days, a stupid thing that had now come in handy. He smiled.

THE DISCOVERY OF NAINA'S MUTILATED BODY WAS MADE IN the evening by a hotel 'helper' (that's room service, plus housekeeping, plus errands, plus sourcing girls, plus plus), who had gone to the room to enquire if Sirji would like to stay another day, and if so, could he kindly pay in advance.

The hotel's receptionist was thrashed by the cops because he hadn't bothered to check the identity proof the esteemed guest had produced while checking in. It was the passport of a British businessman by the name of David Blake, which Sushant Singh later discovered had been misplaced by the owner months ago on a visit to India. And Blake was in Leeds at the time of the murder. The description provided by the hotel staff was this: A tall foreigner wearing sunglasses.

This information had sent Singh and his colleagues on a wild goose chase as they spent days and weeks trying to trace a foreigner. The cop felt a bit foolish when Gloria Gomes mentioned nothing about a handsome blonde. Clearly the Delhi police had been taken for a ride. The Delhi hotel where the crime happened had been forced to shut down once the story broke, but it was back in business ten days later, as it often happens in India.

A FEW WEEKS LATER, WHEN NEWS BROKE OF YET ANOTHER ghastly murder of a young woman in Bangalore, all hell broke loose because the killer's modus operandi was similar. The mystery man had struck a third time in six months, and the media went ballistic. Some members of parliament brought up the issue of multiple murders, and members from the opposition party demanded to know why the killer or killers hadn't been caught yet. The attack on the ruling government was loud and furious, getting the Prime Minister more than worried. He had been battling hard to keep his job, with stories of corruption flooding the media every other day, and didn't really need this shit. He got the Home Minister to issue a formal statement that only said investigations were underway.

Although law and order is a state subject in India, terming it a national crisis, the Home Minister broke protocol and summoned the Delhi and Mumbai crime branch chiefs and police commissioners to his office. He demanded to know details of the headway they had made in the murders, and was livid on discovering there had been no useful leads so far. With assaults happening across the country, it was decided this had to be a national operation, with one man in charge. Before the Minister could threaten to transfer the case to the CBI, Mumbai's crime branch chief, Jasjit Ahluwalia, brought up the name of Azeem Khan.

"Is he the same officer who had nabbed that killer, what's his name?"

"Yes sir. Sainath."

"Are you joking? Hasn't he retired from service?"

"He has. But sir, Khan has the talent and skill needed to help us find this murderer. We have done the hard work, but we need a leader who can think differently."

"Do whatever the hell you want, officers. This case has to be cracked really fast; my bloody job is on the line. I want to get the CBI cracking, but they'll start from scratch, and I don't have the luxury of time. I am basically fucked, you understand?" He then spat into the brass spittoon, but missed his mark.

BROWN SUGAR ADDICT SAINATH HAD A FETISH FOR KILLING pavement dwellers. By the time he was apprehended twenty years ago, the man had slaughtered twenty-nine people. For no apparent reason, he would pick a boulder and casually drop it on the victim's head, as he or she slept. And then he would quickly disappear into the darkness. Sainath continued with his murderous orgy in Bombay for over two years, but there had been no serious pressure on the cops or the ministers. Partly because the media hadn't yet boomed in India, and partly because the targets were poor citizens, dregs of society and therefore easily disposable. India is a nation that's deeply class-driven, and beggars find themselves at the bottom of the pyramid. The upper class citizens pretend they don't exist, which is why the investigation had been tardy. Things started moving only after an American journalist picked up the story, which led to the global media playing out the saga of the 'Unsolved Murders of Bombay'. And this had triggered energy into the city police.

ACP Azeem Khan was ordered to crack the case 'ASAP', and his deputy at the time was Jasjit Ahluwalia. Khan went about the chase methodically, which included night patrols, hard interrogation of suspects, seeking information from *khabris* and speaking to pavement dwellers. The efforts proved fruitless, however, and the killer continued to remain untraceable.

And then Khan decided to change the rules of the game. He set up a team of a hundred constables, with a brief to disguise themselves as beggars and 'sleep' on pavements across the city in the company of regulars. Every single night. This went on for days, much to the annoyance of the constables, and then one night Khan got lucky. The killer struck, but the bait was fast asleep, and by the time he came to his senses, Sainath had fled. While this blunder was kept under wraps, it brought a great deal of stress to Khan, making his resolve to catch the culprit even stronger.

Soon the serial killer was caught in action near the Sion circle. The arrest made national news and turned Khan into a hero, the toast of the nation. Ahluwalia was part of the planning process; therefore Khan made it a point to name him in the media conferences, and the former never forgot that gesture. Medical reports confirmed what the police had always suspected: Sainath was a deranged man who killed for fun. He was raised on the pavements and his father had stabbed his wife when Sainath was just five years old. Remorseful, he jumped in front of a local train. None of the other pavement dwellers had come to the boy's aid, and this had scarred little Sainath's mind. When he grew up, random killings on the streets felt like retribution. And because he was well-versed with every nook and cranny of the city, disappearing hadn't been tough.

SAINATH WAS DECLARED MENTALLY UNSTABLE BY A TRIAL court, and therefore the death sentence was ruled out. He was sentenced to spend the rest of his life at Pune's Yerawada Jail under medical supervision, and Khan thought that was the end of the boulder thrower. But it wasn't. Exactly a year after his arrest, Zeenat received a call at home. Her husband was away at work.

"*Kutiya.*"

"What? Who's speaking?"

"*Kya apna aadmi ko hero samajhreli hai? Kutiya.*"

"Who the hell is this?"

The voice at the other end was chilling. "Sainath, *tera baap. Uss madarchod ko bol main tera khubsoorat sar pe patthar girane wala hai. Mera raaste par ek partner hai. Khyal rakhna, kutiya.*"

Despite many assurances from Khan, Zeenat never fully recovered from the trauma. For years together, every other night, she had nightmares of a stone falling on her head. The jail attendant who had 'allowed' Sainath access to a phone had been sacked immediately, but for Zeenat, the torment would last a lifetime. This was the reason Khan was compelled to ask for an early retirement, though he still had a few years to go. Sainath may not have harmed his wife's body, but he had managed to injure her mind.

SOFTWARE ENGINEER ARCHANA SUKUMARAN WAS A MIGRANT in the city, like many others from around the country. She had shifted to Bangalore from her hometown, Kochi, in the year 2007 to be a part of the IT boom. Evenings were usually spent in the company of female friends at the watering hole in the busy Forum Mall. Brought up in a conservative family, Archana had found it tough to adapt to the new lifestyle. For the first few years, the introvert girl kept to herself, only indulging in the occasional dinner out with her colleagues. And she was shocked to hear of the sexcapades of her Domlur 'chummery' chums. In this arrangement, three, sometimes even four or five working girls jointly rent out an apartment to save on expenses.

The Kochi girl had always thought wild affairs happened only in adult movies. And Archana almost had a nervous breakdown when hundreds of used condoms were discovered in the office parking lot one fine Monday morning. It had taken many calls from the top bosses to keep the media from reporting the story.

Archana had stayed focused on her work, and the pressure of sending fifty per cent of her income back home to her retired parents and a school-going brother always played on her mind. She had had no time or desire for fun with men. Not just invites to date, she would brusquely turn down marriage proposals, even those recommended by her parents. And it had paid off. In six years, the engineer had climbed up the hierarchy to head the software design team. Her income had shot up, and Archana could now rent out a pad for herself in up-market Indiranagar. The Kochi girl had arrived. She now wanted to try her hand at dating.

GEETA WAS IN HER OFFICE. DESPITE A TIGHT DEADLINE FOR A billboard design, and client servicing executives breathing down her neck, her mind was preoccupied. She would get petrified each time her cell phone rang.

"What if it's *him* again? Should I have shared that phone call with the cop? Was it a good idea to conceal the information? Have I fucked up?"

The call had come from a landline phone. Geeta had almost ducked it, thinking it to be an offer of a bank loan. Or worse, that pesky girl from the marriage bureau where her doting parents had registered Geeta's name without seeking her permission. She had spent the last few nights wishing it had been one of the two. Instead, she had heard a gruff, threatening voice, on the night following Imogen's murder; a murder she wasn't aware of at the time.

"Hey Geeta, I am Imogen's boyfriend."

"Er... hi. Do I know you?" She was surprised; her pal hadn't mentioned anything about a boyfriend.

"Hasn't she told you about me?"

"No! What's your name anyway?" Geeta replied half-amused, at the thought of needling Imogen over her dirty little secret.

"Fuck all that. Now listen to me very carefully. If she's told you anything about me, and if you ever reveal my name to the cops, I will come and slit your pretty little neck. And after that, I shall go and lynch your folks in Nagpur."

The call was disconnected even before the half-smile on the receiver's face evaporated. Geeta was dazed and her first move, after she had regained her composure, was to call Imogen. There was no answer. And she tried the number repeatedly through the night with the same result.

A couple of days later, she got the news of her roommate's gory end. Geeta was in a state of panic and yet, she did briefly consider reporting the call. But the menacing voice kept ringing inside her head like a terrible ad jingle.

"If you ever reveal my name to the cops, I will come and slit your pretty little neck. And after that, I shall go and lynch your folks in Nagpur."

Geeta had decided to keep her mouth shut. If this stranger knew where her parents lived, he needed to be hugely feared, and since Imogen had been murdered, even more so. It hurt that she wasn't aware her friend and roommate was having an affair. All Imogen had mentioned in passing was having met someone interesting, but that it was too early to talk about. In other words, Geeta was screwed despite having been kept in the dark. Screwed if the cops found out about her lie, and screwed if she squealed about the call.

"If you ever reveal my name to the cops, I will come and slit your pretty little neck. And after that, I shall go and lynch your folks in Nagpur."

Geeta wiped her sweat and tried to focus on the billboard design. That voice, it meant business. It wouldn't go away from her head.

THE NIGHT RIDE TO GOA HAD BEEN FUN. DARIUS HAD smuggled in a bottle of rum wrapped in a newspaper, and the two, fortunate to have been allotted the last row in the air-conditioned bus, made merry all the way. Imogen needed to get drunk very badly. It wasn't every day that she zipped off on a whim to Goa with a man she had met only a week ago.

Even back home in London, she might have taken a longer time. Large sips of neat Old Monk helped relax her nerves. Darius would occasionally slip his wandering hand into her bra cup, and she would quickly move it away. After a couple of hours, Imogen gave up the resistance and decided to go along. She rationalised that she liked this guy, that there would be sex in Goa, so it didn't make sense to play touch-me-there-not.

Of course, she hadn't paid much attention to the exchange between the bus conductor and her hot date. The man had approached Darius and rudely enquired about what they were drinking, but had left soon thereafter. Darius had aggressively shoved his middle finger right into the chap's bulging belly. The conductor had decided it would be a good idea not to poop this private party.

As soon as the bus reached Goa, Darius broke the alarming news.

"Sorry hon, didn't want to worry you during the journey. I had called my pal just before we started out and he's zipped off for a family holiday to the Ajanta and Ellora Caves."

"And so, now *what*?" Imogen wasn't really thrilled. She liked unpredictable men, but not those who were disorganised.

"Chill, no need to panic. I've heard of this cool resort at Baga, and we could try for a room there. It's not very expensive, and a friend who stayed there last month said the owners don't mind guests indulging in funny business." Darius winked.

"Whatever." She was more keen to rush to the loo, and it had been hurting a bit down there. Darius's long, restless fingers had been busy all night.

AZEEM KHAN WAS SURPRISED BUT DELIGHTED TO SEE THE heavily-built Sikh gentleman standing at the door of his bungalow. It had been some years since he had met his ex-colleague, and the two hugged warmly. Zeenat arrived and joined her husband in welcoming Jasjit Ahluwalia, though her heart did miss a beat when she first spotted the officer.

"Sir, what a delight to meet you after so long! How have you been?" Zeenat went off to get the drinks organised. She didn't need to be told whisky would be the item of choice to celebrate this grand reunion.

"Jasjit, please don't call me that. I'm a civilian now and a newly-minted farmer."

Ahluwalia broke into a hearty laugh. After the pleasantries were over and a few pegs consumed, the very busy crime branch chief came to the reason behind his sudden arrival at the sleepy hill station. And this was what Zeenat had been worried about all along.

"Khan, we badly need your help. There's a dangerous serial killer on the loose. He's already murdered three young women, and we have no bloody clue about this man."

It was Azeem Khan's turn to laugh. "You have to be joking, Jasjit. I'm done with all this, you know that."

Ahluwalia painfully explained the sequence of events, and mentioned that the home ministry had begun to apply serious pressure. He also angrily spoke about the heated debates on national television. Everyone was making fun of the police, every single evening.

"Our honour is at stake, boss, we have to catch the killer immediately. Also, Khan, it's only a matter of time before he strikes again, and you know that."

Zeenat poured some Teacher's into her glass, though she usually hated whisky; white wine was more her thing. She was beginning to get edgy, and wanted this conversation to be over.

"What do you want me to do? I can only pray that the culprit is caught very soon."

"Khan, we really need your help on this one. We need a man who can tackle this differently, one who can think ahead of the killer. We want you to do a Sainath on this. Please don't say no; the life of another innocent is in your hands. This is a very evil man, and he's very smart."

The retired cop took a large gulp, and glanced in the direction of the missus, who was now looking very nervous and pissed drunk. He turned back to his ex-colleague.

"No man, I don't want to be a part of this. I have moved on."

JEROO HAD BEAMED WITH PRIDE WHEN THE SCHOOL TEACHERS told her that Darius was an exceptionally gifted child. Encouraged by the math teacher, she took her son for an IQ test. The result had stunned the already-impressed faculty. A score of 150. This lad was a genius.

Genius. The word had brought a rare smile to Jeroo's face. There had been very little to cheer about in her life, but Darius's IQ score made her feel temporarily optimistic about the future. That evening she gifted herself a new dress, and had dinner at the very expensive (by her standards) Delhi Darbar restaurant with Master Bright, though she could afford none of these. It was also the last time she found any reason to be happy.

A few days later, one neighbour loudly complained that Darius had defecated right outside her door. No, she did not have proof, but she knew it was him because of the way Master Bright laughed in her face when they met at the local *kirana* shop. Of course, Jeroo gave the bitter lady a good shouting, but the downward slide in her life had well and truly begun.

One month later, the building's tottering old watchman woke up to chewing gum paste decorated on his hair. And a week after that, a resident's dog had been found singed with cigarette burn marks. No one could prove it was Jeroo's son's handiwork, but they all knew it was.

And so did the mother. Darius scored high marks in the ninth standard exam. But the smile from Jeroo's face was long gone.

ONE OF THE HASH GANG MEMBERS' SISTER WAS GETTING married in Bangalore, at the Holy Trinity Church. It had been an arranged marriage, and the groom was from that city. Over smokes, Savio D'Souza graciously invited his pals to the wedding. And was particularly keen that Darius came along as he knew the crazy man would make the boring event come to life. Savio had always loathed going to weddings, but this one he could not duck. He needed an antidote.

It took some convincing before Savio agreed to sponsor Darius's train fare. The stay at a relative's house in Ulsoor was going to be free anyway, so it wasn't a huge dent on his pocket. The wages working as a travel agent's assistant weren't much, but a ticket for the general compartment on the Udyan Express he could afford.

And Darius was already itching for some action. The thought of killing in a brand new city was exhilarating. He was enjoying this immensely; Delhi, Goa and now Bangalore. The cops would go mad, he laughed to himself. Darius hadn't watched television in years, nor did he read newspapers, so he wasn't in the know of the frantic chase for the serial killer. He didn't even care; he was too busy having fun. And he knew he was smarter than the cops he often encountered at the Colaba Police Station on account of assorted misdemeanours. One of which had involved a heavily drunk and stoned Darius grabbing a young movie-goer's breasts outside Eros theatre. The boyfriend hadn't been amused; fisticuffs were followed by a night in the lock-up.

IT WAS A CHANCE ENCOUNTER AT ST MARK'S ROAD. THE wedding was scheduled for the evening, and earlier in the day, Darius had sauntered off alone for a meal at the Airlines Hotel. He hailed an auto rickshaw to get to Russell Market, where his contact had asked him to wait for some nice weed.

As soon as a rick halted close to where he was standing, a dusky and very attractive young woman jumped into the vehicle. It was Darius who had flagged down the rick; anyone in his place might have been furious at the rudeness of the trespasser. Instead, he was delighted. Darius instinctively knew this was the woman he'd like to date on this trip, and he'd just got the lucky break he needed.

"Hello my dear lady, do you mind, I stopped this guy!"

In one action, Darius had shoved his head into the rickshaw, so that the driver couldn't move an inch.

"Did you? Well, that's just too bad, I'm taking him now. Look for another one."

Archana, after all these years of living alone and chasing corporate dreams in the big city, had become hardened. Some years ago, the shy Kochi girl might have sheepishly slunk out of the rickshaw when confronted by a tall, aggressive stranger. But that was not going to happen today. She was in charge.

"Hey, that's not fair, I've been waiting like a moron for half an hour, and I need to urgently visit an ailing friend. Where are you headed anyway?"

"Indiranagar."

"Wow, that's a superb coincidence; my pal lives there. Listen, why don't I travel with you, and we split the fare? That would be perfect, don't you think?"

Bangalore rickshaw drivers are crude at the best of times. Irritated by the banter, the man itched to spit out abuse, but felt intimidated by this particular man, and he wisely chose to lie low.

Archana hesitated just for a moment; she had heard of girls being molested inside Bangalore rickshaws, but then nodded in agreement. It was high noon, and this chap looked like a decent and educated sort. Darius smiled. He had this effect on women; they simply couldn't resist him.

The young techie had no idea of the horror she had just invited into her happy, contented and successful life.

JASJIT AHLUWALIA HAD WALKED AWAY A DRUNK AND DEJECTED man. He had tried his best to convince Khan, but the final answer was a clear negative. Back in the ancient guest house run by an elderly couple, a place where milk for preparing tea arrived only at 10 a.m., he gave the issue more thought.

"Without Khan's help, we will be in a soup. The police force would need luck to catch this murderous man. And if one more woman gets slaughtered, a number of heads will roll with her, mine included." Desperate, he decided to employ Plan B. He called Khan's house.

"Zeenat bhabhi, I need to speak with you in private for a few minutes. Can we meet at my guest house?"

"Jasjit, I know what you want, and Khan has already given you his answer. And it's a big no. Forget about it, leave us in peace."

Ahluwalia was aware of his old friend's love for the wife. On many of those nights chasing criminals, Khan had shared his deep affection for Zeenat; he said he'd die if anything happened to her. He also recalled Khan would often land up at home with flowers for no reason at all.

He knew if he could convince Zeenat, getting Khan would be much easier.

"For old times' sake, as a personal favour, give me a few minutes. After that, I shall quietly accept whatever you say and leave for Mumbai immediately. You can't decline the request of a brother."

Zeenat was an emotional sort, a woman with a fragile heart. Ahluwalia had pressed the right button, and without informing Khan, she went over to meet him. The officer belted out gory details of the way the three young girls had been murdered. He then spread out pictures of their mutilated bodies. Zeenat turned away in disgust after the second image.

"You know, they could have been your children, my children. The man has killed thrice, and he is going to strike again. By now, he must have become even more confident. We need Khan for this job, and it's my personal assurance to you nothing will happen to him."

Zeenat knew such assurances counted for nothing. If Sainath could manage to call her from inside a high security prison, anything was possible. But her heart had already begun to melt, and her mind drifted to the trauma the parents would be going through. A call from an imprisoned serial killer had badly shaken her. These people were living the nightmare. Zeenat interrupted Ahluwalia, no longer interested in his sales spiel.

"Okay, let me talk to him. I can promise you nothing, though; it's his call."

"Thank you, dear Zeenat bhabhi. That's all I wanted to hear."

THE CHURCH WEDDING HAD GONE OFF SWIMMINGLY. SAVIO'S elder sister was delighted that a few of his pals from Mumbai made the effort to be there on her big day. She approved of them; they seemed like nice guys. Flavia had always assumed Savio's pals would be a bunch of wastrels and losers, pretty much like her brother. There was a great deal of drinking and dancing at the post marriage reception party. To cut down on expenses, the bash was held at the groom's best friend's bungalow in Sarjapur Road. And as expected, Darius was in full flow; he was the man of the moment, and the groom quietly fell into insignificance.

He danced with every lady in the room, and ensured no one went home without shaking, including the much exhausted grannies. His rambunctious laughter got everyone in high spirits. Savio was the one smiling the most. His investment in the general class seat of Udyan Express had paid off.

Later at night, back in their temporary abode, the Mumbai hash gang gathered for smokes. As the general chatter and gossip went around, Darius put out a totally unexpected request.

"Dude, can I stay at this house for a few more days? Just a few more days, promise. I ran into this creative director from that ad agency J. Walter Thompson, who I know through another pal. He said they are hiring, and asked if I'd like to meet his team for a chat on Wednesday. Savio, please help me bro. I need a job man, you know that!"

Savio, despite being heavily stoned, knew his pal was fibbing. He had known Darius far too long to think otherwise. But he agreed to speak to the owner of the house anyway; he didn't want to disappoint his buddy. After all, Darius had made the wedding reception rock.

"Okay man, but just a couple of nights. And you won't disturb them or ask for anything. You'll arrange for your own grub. Deal?"

"Deal, man, deal. Cross my heart!"

The gang, of course, had no idea Darius had hugely interesting plans lined up for Bangalore.

ARCHANA SUKUMARAN HAD BEEN EASY PICKINGS AS FAR AS the coffee date went, but to get her to bed would prove a lot tougher. She was a single woman with a good job. She was ready for a relationship, but was a strong believer in luck and destiny. Darius read this characteristic quite early, and used it to his advantage. He had noticed it while they were good-humouredly chatting about their run-in during the rickshaw fracas.

"Admit it, Darius, the rick was meant for me, you piled on!"

By then, Darius had introduced himself as a budding, self-financed, 'offbeat cinema' Bollywood filmmaker, who was looking for interesting locales to shoot in and around Bangalore. The quick visit to the pal, who had recently undergone heart surgery, was something he had to do along the way. And because he didn't really know anyone else in the city, could Archana kindly help him?

"Don't you think this chance encounter was written, that it is no coincidence?"

Archana had fallen for the line instantly. Moreover, she fancied this guy. He was from another world, a world far removed from information technology, and this she had found enormously appealing. And she found no harm in providing some tips to a new filmmaker,

"Hell, my name could appear in the opening credits; my parents would be so thrilled." She had secretly smiled.

"Hmm okay, I'll help you."

"Super, thank you already. I feel blessed! Can I meet you later for coffee and discuss the project in detail? How does 3 p.m. work?"

"Okay, cool. There's a Café Coffee Day at 100 Feet Road. It will be easy to find."

Darius felt it was time to leave before the girl changed her mind. She looked the judgemental sort, who could react negatively to an off-the-cuff remark, and Darius was quite notorious for those. Not all women were like Imogen, cool and chilled out. They had reached Indiranagar, he spotted from a road sign. He asked the driver to stop.

"Hey, I'll alight here. Need to pick some flowers for my ailing friend. He lives nearby, so I'll walk. Catch you later!"

And two hours on a lazy Sunday evening was more than enough time Darius had needed to nail this judgemental chick. Archana was floored. She hadn't even dreamed of running into such an interesting, well-read, effervescent stranger. Her colleagues at the IT company were boring geeks, and Darius was the breath of fresh air she could not resist. Yes, she'd love to see him again, and yes, she'd take a day off to do a recce trip with him.

Archana had thought to herself: "Lady, you are ready for a man in your life, and God has dropped this hot potato right into your lap. Try and grab it before it's too late. Don't worry about how your parents will react. There will be plenty of time later to worry about that."

DARIUS'S FIRST ENCOUNTER WITH STREET VIOLENCE HAD happened at the age of eighteen. Until then, he had been focused on his studies, and loved outsmarting fellow students, which usually accompanied sniggering right into their inferior faces. That he could intellectually challenge students senior to him at college was the bigger high. Aside from that, he would indulge in juvenile mischief. But one evening, something brand new happened at the Gateway of India.

He was chatting with his date, a girl he had met at Colaba Market, in the garden facing the monument. Those were days when Bombay was terror-free, and visitors could not only chill inside the garden area, they could hang out, even smoke, right inside the domed structure.

All of a sudden, two goons accosted them, and one pulled out a kitchen knife. They looked the sort who might reside in the slums of Cuffe Parade. Darius's immediate reaction was to freeze, as his panicked friend reached for her purse and quickly parted with the hundred-buck note she was carrying. All he could manage was to stare motionlessly at the muggers, as if his bright brain had short-circuited. The incident transported Darius into the Big Bad Real World, a world far removed from academic scores and college debates. Encouraged by no reaction from the male partner, the robbers, in full view of other visitors, mainly lower middle class families, took turns to molest the girl, while laughing loudly. And then they walked away, like nothing had happened. Darius never met the girl again.

That night, as Darius chain-smoked all the way home, he experienced a remarkable transformation. All along he had thought winning was about beating the opponent in a discussion. But this was new, this was different, and there was no way he was going to be licked at it. One thing Darius hated more than his mother's constant carping was the thought of losing to another man. From the next day onward, every evening, he began to haunt the Gateway. After a week, he spotted the duo.

As soon as the boys came face to face, moving with agility that surprised even Darius, he whipped out the knife from the attacker's pocket, and in a flash, slashed their stunned faces, leaving deep cuts. And then he did something unbecoming of a student who had read the finest English literature. He spat at the slum dogs in their own language.

"Madarchodon, meri ladki ka paisa lootega? Meri ladki par haath daalega? Next time seedha gaand mein ghusa dega."

Darius carelessly slipped the blood red blade into his own pocket, and left the scene, walking very slowly, as if challenging his rivals to attack him from the rear. The two boys were not spotted at the Gateway of India again. And the winner retained the knife as a memento; a memento he stored in the creaky old cupboard. It was a memory of the moment when a studious lad transformed into a violent man.

MUCH LIKE THEIR MUMBAI, GOA AND DELHI COLLEAGUES, THE Bangalore cops were floundering around for clues. The young techie's body, with her severed limbs, had been found in a secluded spot inside the Bannerghatta National Park. It had been discovered by a park official on his daily rounds. The frightened chap thought the lady had been attacked by an edgy leopard, a beast that killed for fun rather than hunger. He was close to the truth.

Inspector Basavraj, who was the first to arrive at the scene, also thought the same. But the forensics team reported that it had been the handiwork of a human being. They also confirmed the similarities with the recent murders in the other cities – dried semen on the face, and a crude object hanging out of the corpse's genitals. It was later identified as a wooden rod.

The news went viral, and the national media leapt into action all over again. Sushant Singh and Rakesh Kamble were briefly excited. Both considered a trip to Bangalore, but later had second thoughts. It was best to lie low on this one. It was most likely to reveal nothing, as in the past. Best to let the Bangalore cops rack their brains and dirty their fingers.

There were protests outside the Karnataka Chief Minister's residence, as well as outside the Parliament House in Delhi. Effigies of the Home Minister were burnt. There was panic on the streets. The serial killer was out of control, and no Indian city was safe.

As expected, the Bangalore cops came up with nothing sensational. The dead girl was identified, and interrogation of her colleagues, friends and neighbours at Indiranagar revealed nothing. A hard-working executive, no fiancé, no boyfriend, and no one-night stands. She was last spotted by a neighbour on the morning of her death, hailing a rickshaw. Her cell phone record indicated Archana had been moving about in the city all day, and after a hard search, the police tracked down the rickshaw she had hired for the day. Yes, there was a man with her. Yes, he was tall and muscular. Yes, he wore glares and a baseball cap. And yes, the asshole hadn't paid. The autorickshaw driver vomited a volley of swear words in Kannada, and some more under his breath, after the cops went off without tipping him for the information.

It was the same man.

But there was collateral damage this time. Unable to deal with the trauma, Mrs. Sukumaran hanged herself from the ceiling fan in her Kochi home, energising the media even further.

PICTURES OF THE MUTILATED BODIES BEGAN TO HAUNT Zeenat. She and Khan did not have a child of their own and sometimes, when she was alone, she would wonder if they had made the right decision. Zeenat would feel a tinge of jealousy when neighbours in Coonoor boasted about how their sons and daughters were doing exceedingly well in the big cities, but she'd quickly ignore the emotion.

It's not that they hadn't tried, but two miscarriages later, the Khans had chosen to abort the idea. In any case, why add to the nation's already booming population, they had rationalised, as most couples in their situation would do. And Zeenat would remind herself they had made the prudent choice given her husband's dangerous career. After Sainath's call, she felt even more convinced they had made the right decision. She wouldn't have been able to handle it if the call had been made to her daughter.

Perhaps it was because she felt these girls were the daughters she never had. Or perhaps it had to do with her conscience. Whatever it was, Zeenat brought up the matter with her husband at dinner.

"Try and help them, Khan. These gruesome murders have to be stopped."

"Yes, I was thinking about it, but I have left that career behind, remember?"

"It's okay. I know you declined the request because you think I won't approve. Well, I'm asking you to help them, just this one time. Please."

The truth is, Azeem Khan had been hoping his wife would make that call. He really didn't wish to worry her any more than he had already done in the past. He was secretly happy to hear the words from her, but didn't show it. However, Khan had one doubt.

"The other problem is, I worked in an era when crimes did not involve technology. Things have changed so much now. They need a younger mind to grapple with today's criminals."

Zeenat lied. Like her husband, she hadn't cared to keep in touch with the news. It was Jasjit Ahluwalia who had shared the information.

"I was reading up a bit in the club library. Leave alone technology, this murderer doesn't even use a cell phone. Khan, this is right up your old-world street, a tech dinosaur like you will do perfectly." She managed a faint smile.

The ex-crime officer knew there were no more excuses left to be given. The apple farm, the winter chill, the mint tea, the Vat 69 – they would all have to wait. He needed to move fast. Instinct told Khan the serial killer would strike again. He seemed to have started having fun. A lot of fun.

JUST AS DARIUS HAD SUSPECTED, THE JUDGEMENTAL GIRL FROZE the moment he reached out for her hand, as the two sat a bit closer in the hired rickshaw. A bit too close for the rick driver, who would repeatedly stare into the rear view mirror hoping to catch some action.

The two had done a recce for the filmmaker's shoot all morning. They had travelled to various spots across the city, and it was late afternoon as the rickshaw headed for Bannerghatta National Park, the last destination for the day.

During the conversations that had happened so far, Archana decided this man was someone she'd really like to get to know better. Even as she was providing location suggestions, her mind was buzzing with other thoughts.

"Here's the problem: This guy lives in Mumbai. Therefore, getting to know him better would be tough. Of course, he would be shooting in Bangalore at some point, so that would provide opportunities. But how would mom react to a man like this? She'd get a heart attack."

But when he reached out for her hand, and the touch told Archana this wasn't just a friendly gesture, the Kochi girl in her came to the fore, and she was stunned. The last time a male had held her hand was back in her college days, when she briefly dated a few boys, and holding hands was all she would permit after months of 'dating'.

"Listen, I'm not comfortable with this."

Darius badly wanted to send a flying kick on her little nose. This was one aunty reaction he had loathed all his life.

"Can't these bloody aunties come up with a better fuck-off line?" But in that one instant, his doubt got confirmed. Getting this aunty into a seedy hotel room was not going to happen, and he didn't have all the time in the world. He had to quickly check out of Savio's uncle's apartment. They had already started politely enquiring about his travel plans. Darius suddenly ached for Imogen. "Why can't all women be like her?"

He quickly calculated Bannerghatta was his best bet. His only chance. The job had to be finished there; it was now or never. "This asshole aunty might not even agree to meet me again."

The rickshaw driver glanced at the meter as his passengers walked off into the park. He was delighted with the reading, and with the usual one and a half time 'surcharge', he would pocket a neat sum tonight. Little did he know he would never see the two again, and that he would never receive his fare.

JASJIT AHLUWALIA AND AZEEM KHAN RODE TO BANGALORE together. The former had already organised the tickets for Mumbai, as he had been sure Zeenat would talk Khan into it. Khan used the nine-hour drive to get a complete debrief from the crime branch chief.

His initial reaction was one of amazement. This guy, who used simple glares, wigs and hats to disguise himself, had managed to evade policemen from around the nation. At the same time, it was an alarming thought. Khan quickly realised this wasn't going to be an easy one to crack; the killer was obviously inventive, super confident, and was thinking ahead of the cops. This was no Sainath from the streets. Considering the profile of the three dead women, they were dealing with an intelligent white collar criminal. But why was he damaging the girls? Why wasn't he raping them with his own organ? And why sever the limbs? Khan's mind was buzzing with questions.

As they boarded the aircraft to Mumbai, Khan decided he'd hit the ground running. They'd head straight for the crime branch office, and get down to work. Coonoor was already a distant memory.

As soon as the aircraft landed, he called his wife.

"Zeenat, this might take many days. Take care, and keep an eye on the farm. Insha'Allah, we'll nab this man before he strikes again."

"Insha'Allah."

ON THE PRETEXT OF SEARCHING FOR AN EXOTIC LOCALE, Darius led his companion deeper into the woods. Even as Archana marvelled at the beauty of nature, he kept a sharp look-out for civilisation, while regaling the lady with his ready wit. Enjoying the company, the park, and a day away from the stuffy office workstation, she didn't realise how deep they had moved in. When they reached a thick shrub, Darius laughed out loudly.

"What's so funny?"

"Aunty, you are sweet but really dumb, just like all other Indian women. You should never have come with me, you moron!"

Archana had no time to react to this sudden transformation in her companion. Though she must have been shocked that instant, her body had been found with her eyes wide open. A really heavy object came crashing down on her head, cracking her skull.

Soundlessly and effortlessly, Darius went about his now familiar ritual. He then walked out of the park from another direction, in order to avoid running into that cheating rickshaw driver.

"Just another tourist," other visitors who passed by him might have thought.

That evening, he wished Savio's relatives a warm good-bye with a bunch of flowers he had plucked from the park. The man of the house was happy to see the freeloader go. He had been worried the visit would stretch further.

"Son, hope your stay was fruitful."

"Very fruitful, sir, very!"

AT THE CRIME BRANCH OFFICE, THE RETIRED OFFICER WAS allocated a corner room to himself. Ahluwalia knew he needed to provide Khan with a quiet place to think and keep his mind away from matters related to routine investigations. And *thinking* was what had been missing all along; the cops had only been *doing*, and that hadn't worked. The way Khan had managed to nab Sainath was still discussed with admiration in the crime branch office.

Khan asked for Rakesh Kamble and Sushant Singh to be made available. Kamble was, of course, already around, but a special request had to be sent to the chief of the Delhi crime branch to spare Singh for a few days. Khan didn't ask for investigating officers from Goa or Bangalore, choosing to meet them later, if needed. The idea was to constitute a small team, share findings and ideas, and hope to discover some sort of a clue. Meanwhile, Khan began decorating the soft board, his usual starting point while investigating serious crimes.

He tore a large sheet of paper into different pieces, scribbled notes on each, and put them up. This is what he had gathered so far from discussions with Ahluwalia.

Hard object used to smash the victim's head.

No rape, but strange objects being used for penetration.

Limbs chopped off.

Ejaculation on the face, before or after death.

Young women, all in their twenties.

Different cities.

Killer is a Luddite. Perhaps.

Tall, powerfully built, perhaps in his late twenties/early thirties.

White collared, perhaps a corporate executive or a businessman.

Killing for pleasure, not money.

Khan stepped back and stared at the soft board.

'Ejaculation on the face' was bothering him. He scratched his head. "Why would anyone, however insane, do such a creepy thing?"

KAMBLE AND SINGH WERE EXPECTED IN HIS OFFICE THE NEXT morning. Having arrived very early to work, Khan scanned the net to suss the media reports. He was amused by the wild theories being belted out by columnists and so-called opinion makers. He half-smiled, thanking God that in his days one didn't have to put up with this bullshit. He also wondered if the killer was following the media. "White collar criminal. He must be."

He learnt from the morning newspapers that his arrival had been leaked to the media. A tad annoyed, Khan thought of taking it up with Jasjit. It was too damn early, he hadn't even had time to think clearly, but he changed his mind. Sooner or later, the journalists would find out anyway; best to stay focused on the investigation.

Singh and Kamble walked in together. And the hour-long discussion told Khan that no headway had been made despite enormous field work. He realised the crime branch sleuths had done nothing wrong; they had gone by the book, and this was why they had lost the plot. This killer was a different creature altogether; the standard methods wouldn't work. Also, Khan, from his own policing experience, could see that the two officers weren't comfortable being placed in the same room. A little ego massage was required, and the oil would be a lie.

"Let's work as a team from here on. I asked for you guys because Ahluwalia has been singing your praises. This guy is going to kill again. It's only a matter of time, so let's get him before that."

"Yessir!" Both replied in unison, though they felt weird working under a retired officer. But they were delighted all the same, because now it wasn't their asses on the line anymore; it was Khan's.

"Kamble, this girl Geeta Kulkarni. Bring her here, let's chat with her again."

Kamble could have called Geeta, but he decided to pick her up. He liked visiting the ad agency office; the girls looked pretty hot.

IT'S NOT THAT JEROO HADN'T TRIED TO FIX THINGS. A COUPLE of years ago, having found that her son was behaving increasingly abnormally, she had forced him to meet a shrink. This was made possible by a distant cousin who lived in Ahmedabad. Gentle and soft-spoken, Homi seldom visited Mumbai, and even on the rare occasions that he did, he would steer clear of Jeroo's house. That's because on a visit some years ago, Darius had accosted him at a bakery shop, grabbed his wallet, and cleaned it of all its contents without a thank you. Homi had no desire to be an ATM for losers. He made limited income through his little medical retail shop. But gentle Homi knew the lad needed help, and could not resist offering it.

"Meet Dr. Dushyant Desai. He runs a clinic near Opera House. Give him my name, and he won't charge you a penny. I had helped him once and he remembers."

More than the desire to sort out her son's messed-up mind, the offer of a free treatment had appealed to Jeroo. And surprisingly, Darius readily agreed to the idea. Little did she know that her son had been bored for a few days and was looking for action, and that she had just provided it to him on a platter.

Inside the consulting room, the conversation was punctuated with Darius's hysterical laughter; laughter that prompted a middle-aged patient seated in the waiting room to contemplate a hasty getaway.

"Darius, how did your day go today? What did you do?"

"Well, I didn't fuck anyone, if that's what you're asking. Chicks are in short supply these days. Did you, doctor? Still find Mrs. Desai sexy?"

Stunned, the doctor tried hard to remain composed. He was used to meeting mad men, but no one had been this abusive before.

"Relax, son! I know you are not happy being here. But you will be in some time."

"What do you charge per hour?"

"Ah, don't worry about that, let's talk about you."

"Five hundred bucks? Thousand bucks? You charge that kind of moolah from mind-fucked people to ask them what errands they ran during the day? Wow, that's such a cool job!"

"Darius, we have to focus on *your* life, and I can help you."

"Really? Can you swear on the god staring down at us from your wall?"

"Let's keep gods out of this. Let me try to help you, please."

"Great. Give me a thousand bucks, I need to party tonight. Now that's the kind of help I really need."

"What's troubling you, young man? Please tell me." The usually affable doctor was now beginning to lose it.

"You know what's troubling me? It's the thought of you cheating pricks called shrinks. You talk complete crap with idiots for an hour, and then attack their wallets. You scumbags are thieves, blood-sucking insects. What are you thinking right now, how are you feeling right now, what do you like, what do you dislike? Bloody hell, I'd do that shit for free!"

"Cool it mister, that's no way to talk. I will have to ask you to leave."

"Guess what? That's exactly what I want to do, man. Don't want to mess my mind discussing life with a dolt like you."

Before the psychiatrist could react, Darius leapt for the man's bald head, and grabbed it tightly with one hand. With the other, he pulled out a knife and held it to the doctor's throat.

"Dude, you speak about this to anyone, I will fry your *taklya* head. And then check if anything's going on inside."

More laughter.

"And thanks for the consultation, Dr. Desai. That was very useful!" He then emptied the doctor's wallet.

Dr. Dushyant Desai suffered a massive heart attack that evening. With his death, Jeroo's last hope of a better future for her high IQ son died too. She had a lurking feeling Darius had been behind the doctor's sudden demise, but wisely chose not to discuss it with her son.

Instead, she returned to doing the only thing she knew – curse her rotten luck.

A NERVOUS GEETA WAS ESCORTED INTO KHAN'S ROOM. WITH three cops staring intently at her, the young woman began to sweat despite the whirring room air-conditioner. Khan tried to make her comfortable.

"Geeta, sorry to have pulled you out of office, my apologies."

Politeness wasn't what she had expected. Geeta's experience with Kamble had prepared her for hard talk. She began to breathe a bit more normally. "No problem sir. What can I do for you? Inspector Kamble has already spoken to me."

Kamble responded sternly. "Boss wants to ask more questions, so kindly cooperate."

Khan ignored him. "I know this is tough on you, but can you go back in time once again, Geeta? Did Imogen Parsons drop any hint, even a faint hint, about a new friend? Think carefully, there's no hurry." He rang the buzzer and asked for tea to be served immediately.

"No sir. I was shocked to hear she went to Goa with someone on a holiday. She said she was travelling on work."

"Can you try and guess who the man might be, or where Imogen might have met him? Do you suspect an acquaintance?"

"I'm afraid I don't know. Perhaps she ran into him somewhere. Or he's a friend from the past who reconnected. Maybe someone from the UK. I don't know, sir."

Khan wasn't just listening, he was watching her intently and instinctively knew Geeta was concealing important information. Her eyes were shifty, and she had been fidgeting with the chair. It was possible the killer had tried to contact her. Khan took a shot in the dark.

"And you didn't recognise his voice?"

"No sir, never heard it before."

Singh and Kamble jumped from their chairs. The art director broke into a sweat again, and the teacup slipped from her hand. Geeta realised she had screwed up, and that she had been tricked.

"Why the hell didn't you tell me that before?" Kamble was livid. Singh smiled to himself.

Khan motioned to the officers to sit down. He asked for a fresh cup of tea for the visitor.

"It's okay, Geeta. I know you must have been scared. I don't blame you, this can happen to anyone. Now tell me exactly what he said to you. Every single word."

IT WAS TOO LATE. GEETA'S CALL RECORD SCAN LED TO THE land phone number, which turned out to be a public phone located in Gamdevi. Of course, the attendant could not recollect a thing; they didn't keep an eye on callers. In addition, that call was made days ago, so to jog the chap's memory was a pointless exercise. The constables dispatched for the job were pissed off at their precious time having been wasted. The duo polished off the *vada pavs* from a local hawker's *thela*, and left without paying a paisa. The illegal hawker knew better than to protest.

Geeta's life became miserable after her goof-up at the crime branch. She hadn't yet forgotten the lethal warning:

If you ever reveal my name to the cops, I will come and slit your pretty little neck. And after that, I shall go and lynch your folks in Nagpur.

Of course, she didn't know his name, but the killer didn't know that. And what if the cops managed to establish contact with him, and her name came up? He'd assume Geeta had ratted, and her life would be over. Just like Imogen's.

Unable to focus on her work, she went to the pub located in the adjoining building, and did two things she had never done before. Drink alone. And drink at 4 p.m. After a few large ones, Geeta cursed herself for having chosen Imogen as her roommate. She later called her parents to check if everything was fine at home in Nagpur.

Later in the evening, she did another thing she had never done before. Go to a Hanuman temple.

KHAN, SINGH AND KAMBLE FLEW TO DELHI. KHAN WANTED TO take a look at the room in which Naina's body had been found in multiple pieces. It helped that while the hotel was buzzing again, that particular room had been sealed off. Singh had been a bit irritated when Khan came up with the idea.

"But sir, we investigated the place thoroughly."

"I'm sure. No harm in taking a look again."

The manager-cum-receptionist tried to flee as soon as he spotted Singh, accompanied by two men, barging into the hotel. Malhotra was worried they had come to shut his place down for good, and take him in for interrogation on the other nefarious activities of the hotel; call girls on demand being one of them. Singh chased him down, slapped him a couple of times, and dragged him back into the dingy lobby.

"Open the bloody room. Boss has come from Mumbai to take a fresh look."

Malhotra, half relieved, was only too happy to do the honours.

Expectedly, the room was stinking heavily. Kamble rushed for his handkerchief. There were dried bloodstains on the bed, and on the floor just below the bed. There were no apparent signs of a struggle, and the rest of the furniture seemed to be undisturbed. Khan suspected Naina might have willingly slept on the bed with her assailant. This indicated a degree of trust. But if she had known the man for a period of time, the police investigation would have thrown it up. Not her husband, not the maid, not any of the family members and friends had any idea she was having an affair. The hotel staff had seen her arrive on her own, so it couldn't have been a case of kidnapping. Khan's mind was busy juggling thoughts as he looked for a clue, however minor.

He noticed three cigarette stubs in the rusted metal ashtray. Khan took a whiff and smelt hash. "Hmm, a drug addict."

There were traces of blood in the bathroom, too. The killer must have rinsed the blood from the object used to crush Naina's head. Khan rummaged through the waste bin. Nothing of importance. A beer can and rotting banana peels. This was a clean job.

"Let's go to Goa. Maybe we'll find something there."

Singh was pleased. He had been worried the old man would discover something new, and make him look like a careless fool, just as Khan had done to Kamble. To celebrate the moment, he punched Malhotra in the stomach as they exited the hotel.

"*Behenchod*, next time you let guests in with fake IDs, I shall chop your little *lund* off."

UNLIKE MALHOTRA, GLORIA HAD MOVED ON. THE ROOM HAD been cleaned up; it had been painted, refurbished, redone. She wished to have nothing to do with Imogen's death; she wanted no memory of the incident. Mr. and Mrs. Gomes had turned paranoid. They had begun doing something unheard of in Goa hotels: Demand to know the exact relationship between couples who sought to check in, and in certain cases, they would insist on proof of marriage. Which is why Gloria was extremely displeased to see cops at her doorstep all over again. This wasn't good for business at all. Already, thanks to snide comments on TripAdvisor, the resort had gotten a terrible name. Until that ghastly crime, it was only mosquitoes that guests had cribbed about.

Khan was a little more hopeful than he was in Delhi. This couple looked an educated sort, and Gloria looked like a smart cookie.

"Can you describe the man again, just for my benefit?"

Gloria tried hard to keep calm. "Sir, I have already told the Goa police, and the two gentlemen accompanying you, all that I saw and know. I'm afraid we can be of no further assistance."

A sullen Joaquin nodded in agreement, wisely allowing his wife to deal with this situation, given his ill temper. "These bloody asshole cops, they can't solve the case and they'll continue to torment us," he said to himself.

Khan figured the impatience had more to do with wanting to forget a terrible incident rather than innate impoliteness. He gently prodded her on.

"Mrs. Gomes, please indulge me a bit, this won't take long. Did the two emerge from the room at all? Perhaps for a meal or a snack?"

"No, they checked in very early in the morning. I guess they must have eaten on the way. In any case, we don't offer meals to guests; they have to find their own way. And no, I didn't see them come out of the room."

"And he was gone late at night or early next morning?"

"No idea."

"Okay, Mrs. Gomes, describe the man to me, anything remarkable that you may have noticed about the way he spoke or in his mannerisms."

Gloria tried to recollect. "He was laughing a lot, and the foreigner girl seemed to be enjoying his company. They were a bit, well, touchy-feely, if you know what I mean."

"Did he have a distinct accent?"

"Hmm, no. But he spoke fluent English; must be convent school educated. And his voice was a bit heavy."

"How would you describe him in one word?"

Gloria gave this careful thought.

"Confident. Very confident."

Indeed, that is what Khan had suspected about the serial killer, and it was one description he was hoping not to hear. Confident meant two things: The man was clever, and the chances of his making errors were low. And that he would strike again.

As the disappointed team started to leave, Gloria shouted out from behind them. "And oh, one more thing, officer. While we were dealing with the check-in formalities, I heard the girl say something about someone called Rita or Sita; not sure of the exact name."

KHAN WAS BACK IN HIS OFFICE, STARING AT THE SOFT BOARD. He had not harboured notions of collecting breakthrough clues on his travels, but had hoped to form a better picture of the killer. He needed to understand the man, to try and get to know him a little better. This had to be the starting point in a situation where leads were hard to come by. Khan had bought a Post-It pad, and he started scribbling. He pasted an observation below each of the paper cuttings he had displayed earlier.

Hard object used to smash the victim's head.
Seeks instant death, does not want to torture the victims. Could also be trying to avoid anyone hearing screams.
No rape, but strange objects being used for penetration.
Sadistic tendency. Is he religious? Is this some sort of a pagan ritual? What's the point of this?
Limbs chopped off.
More sadism. Hates women.
Ejaculation on the face, before or after death.
Very odd. The ladies weren't rejecting him, they appeared to be happy to be with him. Perhaps another sign of hating women.
Young women, all in their twenties.
This could be because he is an attractive man, and finds dating easier with young women. He needs to win their confidence so that they agree to meet him in private places.

Different cities.

Is he trying to escape being seen/caught? Or is he trying to prove a point? Perhaps he wants national recognition; most serial killers seek recognition.

Killer is a Luddite. Perhaps.

A tech-challenged sort. Or smart enough not to use a cell phone.

Tall, powerfully built, perhaps in his late twenties/early thirties.

We are dealing with a tough nut. Murders must be easy to execute.

White collared, perhaps a corporate executive or a businessman.

Bad news. The culprit is an intelligent, confident man; he is no hit and run fool like Sainath. We are in trouble.

Killing for pleasure, not money.

More bad news. He's begun to have a blast; there is no clear motive, and he will strike again. VERY SOON.

Khan began to think even as he realised he didn't have enough raw material to work on. The man wasn't leaving behind any clues at all, and so this needed a brand new approach. The retired officer then did something he hadn't done in many years. He called Kamble and asked if he had a cigarette to spare.

"If Zeenat finds out, she will freak out." But he simply had to have a smoke.

DARIUS HOPPED ACROSS FOR BREAKFAST TO KAILASH PARBAT restaurant in Colaba. He liked going there because food wasn't expensive, and he'd often run into European backpackers, which usually led to free smokes. The place was packed this morning. Darius decided to share a table with an obese Sindhi gent, who was busy digging into his Pakwan Dal, while reading a newspaper.

"Old man, don't eat all that crap, it will kill you."

The Sindhi gent looked up from the newspaper, and quickly decided to ignore the uninvited attention.

"Don't want to talk to me, uncle? Don't want to hear the truth? Fat, piggy coward."

Darius was usually gregarious with strangers, and having to spend his meagre resources on food had made him quite cranky today. Worse, there were no European backpackers in the house.

The man, clearly intimidated, but not wanting to create a scene, didn't reply. He glanced around, spotted a vacant slot in another corner, picked up his food and left. Darius burst into hysterical laughter. He wanted to tickle the obese man's jelly belly, but let it go. The guy looked immensely uninteresting anyway. But the fleeing Pakwan Dal consumer had forgotten to carry along his newspaper, and there was no way he was going to return for it. Darius casually picked it up and grinned on reading the headline.

"Retired cop heads investigation. Promises to nab serial killer, claims he has solid leads."

Darius stared at Azeem Khan. "Wow! This is getting interesting."

He shouted out to the obese man, "Sethji, thanks for the newspaper!"

There was no response; the chap had buried his face into the extra bowl of dal he had just ordered. He had prudently decided it was best to let this mad man depart first, lest he run into him outside the restaurant.

KHAN WAS STILL SMOKING KAMBLE'S CIGARETTE WHEN Ahluwalia walked in.

"How was the trip to Goa and Delhi?"

"No real leads yet; we need to investigate harder. Need time."

"And time is what we don't have. The media isn't giving the murders a break as no other scandal has hit the nation. The Home Minister called for the third time today. Poor man sounds quite stressed out."

"Frankly Jasjit, I am a bit worried. We are dealing with a sharp killer here. This is no Sainath. And luck seems to be favouring him; he's getting away with simple bloody disguises."

"Still, we need to speak to the media and need to reassure the women of the nation. They are scared out of their brains, man. The press wants to meet you, so will you address them later in the evening? Just give them the usual bullshit about working hard on the matter, that we'll get the guy soon, blah, blah."

"Hmm, okay, if that's what you want."

Ahluwalia stared at the butt in the ashtray. He looked a bit concerned.

"Khan, be careful. Some bad old habits are best not visited again."

IN HIS YOUNGER DAYS, WHEN THEY WERE IN THEIR LATE thirties, the two had drifted away. Khan desperately wanted to have a child, but it hadn't worked. Even as he took care not to share the emotion with Zeenat, to avoid making her feel like a lesser human being, his mind had wandered.

While Zeenat buried herself in spirituality, her husband found succour in a prostitute. Khan had been attracted to Shraddha, a dancer he had met during a raid on a Santacruz dance bar. The cops had suspected the bar was a pick-up joint, and the suspicion had proved to be accurate. In addition, the bar owner had not cared to keep the beat constables happy. A few days later, when the girls were being bailed out, Khan's eyes fell upon one who didn't look the sort who would be whoring out of choice. She had sad eyes, and she appeared more like a lower middle class housewife who had been forced to trade her body.

"Hey, you there, don't leave. Come here, I need to talk to you." Khan beckoned Shraddha to his desk, as he waved at the constables to lead the others out.

Shraddha reacted like a frightened deer that had been zapped on a national highway by the lights of a lorry zooming in. "Sahib, let me go, please. I have a little one waiting for me at home."

"Don't worry, you are not in trouble. Tell me, why are you doing this? Be honest. Maybe I can help you."

Something about this cop's gentle, caring voice disarmed Shraddha. She didn't have friends she could trust, and had always craved for a shoulder she could cry on. Instinctively, the woman knew she may have found one.

"My husband used to work as an office assistant with a small firm in Govandi. His employer caught him stealing a thousand rupees from the office and in anger, had his right hand chopped off. He is useless now, we have a two-year-old son, and I have to do this to feed three mouths. Please understand, sahib, I beg of you."

Moved, Khan lit a cigarette, jotted down her address and asked the prostitute to leave. Any further interaction would have raised eyebrows. He later visited Shraddha and offered to pay for her child's healthcare and future education. It helped that her husband was not at home at the time. The woman was delighted, and with time, Khan found himself sexually attracted. And soon he began sleeping with her.

It was in those days that Khan had begun chain-smoking and drinking heavily. Perhaps it was his way of dealing with his missing conscience, though he did feel awful about betraying his sweet, loving Zeenat.

The affair with Shraddha had lasted three years, but his wife never found out, as wives seldom do. Although some of his colleagues, including Jasjit, were aware of it. One day the prostitute disappeared from her home, never to be seen again. There were rumours she had been burned alive by her handicapped husband. Khan decided not to hunt her down; he chose to shake off the memories and move on. Perhaps he had been given a chance to end this, he rationalised. As Shraddha receded from his mind, so did the urge to smoke and drink.

And it had reappeared after all these years. Khan was stressed out. He knew there would be a murder very soon, and he could do nothing to stop it. Suddenly he wanted to rush into Shraddha's arms. She knew how to make Khan feel relaxed. And happy.

THE PRESS CONFERENCE WAS NOISY AND DISORGANISED, JUST as most are in India. Young reporters and camera crew members, inadequately trained and often ill-mannered, were tripping over each in order to get a vantage position. A few verbally abused each other, while a couple of photographers came to blows.

Jasjit Ahluwalia, seated next to Khan, ordered the journalists to maintain discipline. It took twenty minutes for everyone to settle down, and then a hand-held microphone was passed around for reporters to fire their questions; one question permitted per individual.

"Mr. Khan, have you made any headway so far?"

"Yes, we have promising clues."

"Why is the police taking so much time to act? Three women have been brutally killed."

"Well, as I said, we have some leads, and are in pursuit of the assailant."

"Is it the same man? Or is it a gang?"

"That we can say only after the first arrest has been made. My hunch is it's the same man."

"No luck with the killer's sketch that was circulated?"

"As I said, we have some clues."

One reporter from a Hindi news channel, trying to score brownie points with her boss, got aggressive. "Aren't the crime branch and the police ashamed of themselves? You people have formed a national team and have nothing to show for it."

"As I said, we have some clues."

Khan had been exposed to such pointless media conferences before, and knew that journalists in India tend to be accusatory rather than inquisitive, with their eyes focused on media rating points, rather than the truth. Which is why he had come prepared to provide the same boring answers without losing his cool. Ahluwalia wasn't a patient man however, and thundered: "Please don't ask the same stupid questions and waste our time. We have more important things to do."

This led to a wave of protests in the room.

Later that evening, the portly TV anchor, not being able to offer anything new to his viewers, decided to go after the cops. He ran an hour-long show titled, 'The useless and arrogant crime branch'.

READING THE NEWSPAPER REPORT, DARIUS FELT A SENSE OF empowerment; he liked all the attention. He had already overheard people on the streets excitedly discuss the killings. His menacing, glares-adorned sketch was in the newspaper. Darius realised the time had come to change his appearance, and he found the prospect of that exciting. But he needed some funding. It was time to borrow again. He was thinking of the next course of action as he sat inside a BEST bus, route No. 123, which travels from RC Church at the southern end of Mumbai to Chowpatty and beyond. From the window seat, he spotted a few monks crossing the road outside Churchgate Station. Darius smiled. "Not bad, eh!"

A man who looked like a daily wage worker boarded the bus and sat down beside him. Darius clasped his nose.

"Abey chutiye, kitne din se nahaya nahin? Baas maarta hai."

The daily wage worker wasn't amused, he turned out to be an equally aggressive sort.

"Oye, tere baap ka gaadi hai kya? Chutiya hoga tu aur tera baap!"

After a few more insults involving their respective mothers and sisters, the two men changed gears and got into fisticuffs. Some passengers panicked, forced the driver to stop and fled from the bus. The two were separated by the bus conductor who threatened to take the bus to the nearest police station. Darius backed off, muttering that there was no need to cause other passengers inconvenience. He shouted an apology at the remaining passengers, alighted from the bus, and from the road, showed his middle finger to the daily wage worker, who by then had triumphantly moved to the window seat. The favour was duly returned.

As the bus sped away, Darius broke into loud laughter. Young couples dating on the Marine Drive promenade turned around to stare nervously. The lovebirds out here are always on the lookout for a sadistic policeman, who'd take immense pleasure in demolishing their 'private moments'. Some years ago, a police constable had gone on to rape one such lovebird, so there is good reason to remain alert.

Darius blew air kisses in their direction, and then shouted at a couple seated closest to where he was standing. *"Oye gaandu, haath kidhar daal raha hai?"* The couple ducked under the parapet.

He then flipped open the daily wage earner's half torn, weather-beaten wallet. And found only five hundred bucks. Livid, he shouted in the direction of the bus which had zipped off to a considerable distance. *"Bhikhari madarchod. Akha time waste kiya."*

Some of the lovebirds fled from the site.

Darius, humming the Beatles song 'Help!', walked in the direction of Churchgate Station and darted into Air Cool Hair Dressers. Jumping the queue, he plonked himself on a chair, and chirpily called out to a barber, who could only stare at him helplessly. *"Takla kar de yaar, naya look try karna hai. Apun ka bad luck chal raha hai."*

A handful of patrons, still awaiting their turn, hopped across to the cashier's desk to lodge a protest. The man, not wanting to create a scene, lied.

"Er, the gentleman has a prior appointment."

He didn't know Darius's name, but from past experience, was aware it was best to keep interaction with this chap to a minimum.

SHRADDHA WAS ALIVE. HER HUSBAND SUHAS HAD FOUND OUT about her extracurricular activities, and had promptly dispatched her to a municipal hospital. With multiple fractures, a broken nose, permanent damage to one eye and severe bleeding from the uterus. It had taken the hapless woman months to recover, and had cost all her savings. Savings she had managed after a great deal of toiling on the bodies of lecherous men.

Suhas had been arrested, but Shraddha refused to file charges. She needed someone to look after her young child while she was in hospital. Also, it was quite possible the violent Suhas would hurt her and their son as retribution. In any case, he had found a job as a courier company's delivery boy, and his income, however lowly, was badly needed to make ends meet.

It had taken Shraddha some years to fully heal. She now worked as a freelance domestic help, catering to multiple households. Lying on the floor inside their slum dwelling, watching the third-hand television set the family had managed to procure, she saw Khan at the press conference. Her heart missed a beat. Shraddha had liked him a lot, mainly because Khan had always been gentle with her. He used to treat her as a human being. And that was something she had never experienced with another man, not even her factory worker father. The emotionally scarred woman thought of reaching out to Khan for financial help; after all, he had offered assistance in the past.

But the thought of how Suhas would react deflated her. They were now in their mid-forties, but the man's rage hadn't receded one bit. And yet, it was a chance she simply had to take. She had to find a way to organise money for her son's future. A dropout from school, unemployed and wild, young Aditya had already begun showing signs of growing up to be his father's spitting image. And that Shraddha certainly did not wish for her son.

"COME ON UNCLE, A FEW THOUSAND RUPEES, JUST TO TIDE things over."

Darius, unknown to Jeroo, was bonding with his paternal uncle, Jahanbux Irani, at Coffee House on Pune's Moledina Road. Irani had severed all ties with his sister-in-law immediately after his brother's death. He had always blamed Jeroo for his brother's early demise. And the lady had instructed Darius never to establish contact with his uncle. Never, ever, she had shouted.

Jahanbux Irani ran a lampshades store on MG Road, and with no children of his own, had saved up enough to lead a peaceful life with his wife. Darius suddenly showed up at his retail outlet. Irani was taken aback, but also happy. After all, this was his dead brother's son, the only child of a brother he had always been fond of. He invited his nephew to join him for a dosa and idli lunch.

"Son, even if I help you now, the money will not go far. You need to find a job, you need to get a life. You can't be loafing around in your thirties. Ronnie would have been ashamed."

"Trust me uncle, I am looking for a job. There have been positive responses, and I shall land up with a good one soon. And then I swear I shall return your money. You know mom is badly broke!"

Jahanbux raised his hand. "Don't mention that wretched woman. I won't lend you a rupee."

Darius said nothing; he knew it was best to shut up, to let the old man have the last word. And he knew, behind the tough exterior, Uncle Jahanbux possessed a generous heart. Darius threw a spoonful of gunpowder chutney into the *sambhar*, and dunked a gobbet into his mouth. It was time to switch on the emotion button.

"Please, uncle. You know dad left me nothing. I have had a tough life. It hasn't been easy. And if your own people don't help you in need, who will?" Gunpowder-induced tears rolled down his eyes.

It worked. Jahanbux Irani and his nephew returned to the lampshades store, where Darius was handed twenty thousand rupees.

"I'm warning you son, don't blow it up on bad habits, else I will never see your face again. Now go away before I remember you are that ugly woman's son, and change my mind."

Darius was only too happy to run; he had work to do. It was time to visit the German Bakery. Have some pastries and masala chai, and remember all those poor souls who had died in the bomb blast. It was also a happy chick-hunting ground. Mind-fucked chicks, just like him.

KHAN WAS SMOKING IN THE POLICE CAR, ON HIS WAY TO THE hotel near Metro cinema where he had been put up, courtesy the crime branch. He had been offered an apartment, but he had declined. A house would have meant he was on a long-haul, a hotel symbolised transit. It subconsciously reminded him that he needed to catch the killer quickly and return home.

And the hotel stay had reassured Zeenat too, who was worried her man would disappear for a long time. Khan called her.

"All well at home?"

"The usual power cuts, but all well otherwise. Don't worry about Coonoor. Your dear farm is being well looked after."

Khan took in a deep drag, hoping Zeenat couldn't hear the sound.

"Hope you aren't stressed out. You looked a bit tired on television."

"Hmm, no, I'm fine. It's just that we haven't got any leads yet, even the *khabri* network has reported nothing so far."

"Have patience, you will catch him soon. I know that. Khan never fails. Do you want me to come over and stay with you for a bit?"

No, definitely not, I have started smoking, honey. Instead, Khan belted out the expected spiel about someone having to look after the apples, him having to travel all the time, etc, etc. And then he disconnected the call.

Not Zeenat, at this point, Shraddha would be the comforting factor he craved. She was a whore, but she understood him. She would have understood Khan needed the smokes right now and she wouldn't nag him.

The retired cop decided to think about something else. Semen on the dead women's faces came back to haunt him. A thought occurred to Khan. Yes, it could be that. He conference-called Kamble and Singh.

"Get teams in Bangalore, Delhi and Goa cracking on local doctors who deal with impotency issues. Let them carry a sketch of this guy. Ask the doctors if they've met anyone who looks like this bastard."

HE TRIED TO STRIKE A CONVERSATION WITH FELLOW PATRONS, but it didn't lead anywhere. The women appeared disinterested in casual chatting, and it took a few rebuffs for Darius to get that the joint had gotten itself a notorious reputation after the bomb blast, and folks had become wary of strangers. It wasn't the German Bakery of the past, where you could hop over to anyone's table and get talking. And then follow it up with some action. It looked different, it felt different. Darius decided to buy a few cigarettes and take a walk to the Osho Ashram.

And then he spotted her, as she experimented with 'Osho slippers' at a Tibetan street vendor. Darius, now looking like an unshaven, skin-head punk, decided to behave cool. An aggressive manner would most likely not go down well with white babes who've travelled all the way to escape the reality of their screwed-up existence.

"Hello there, I suggest you go for the ones laced with beads. I'm told the beads bring good luck." He began trying out a pair for himself.

Sarah glanced at the stranger, and half smiled.

"Always a good start, Darius, always a good start."

The accent was unmistakably Yankee. "Is that so? Wow! Right, then I'll go for a pair of those."

"And by the way, the maroon dress sits well on you, makes you look divine. Such a contrast, you and I: the angel and the devil."

Sarah was now grinning. "You stay in the Ashram? Didn't see you around."

"Nope, they wouldn't let me in. I flunked the AIDS test." Darius broke into his trademark guffaw, and then seized the moment.

"Hi, my name is Krishna, you can call me Krish. I just arrived from Mumbai for a friend's wedding."

"Sarah. I've been here just ten days, and I'm still finding my way around. It's a new experience for me." The Osho disciple was in two minds whether she had made the right journey, and the stranger sensed this immediately.

"No worries, I could be of help, if you permit me. My dad used to be an Oshoite. He was one of Bhagwan's trusted aides, and he lived in the Ashram for twenty years. I could give you some tips, I suppose."

"Oh, that would be wonderful, just the person I wanted to meet!" Sarah was delighted; she had been looking for someone who could give her a lowdown on this strange place. She quickly finished her purchase.

"See, the beaded slippers worked their magic. Come, let's have lunch, I'm famished. I know of this wonderful Thai joint just round the corner. We can walk there."

AN HR MANAGER AT A NEW YORK CITY CORPORATE, SARAH Fisher had decided to spend time at the Osho Ashram to try and find inner peace, and hopefully, discover a new meaning to life. She had been through a string of failed relationships, which had triggered an addiction to sleeping pills. A friend had suggested 'a stint in spirituality', and she had liked the sound of it. Sarah had read about the Ashram in an article published in *The New York Times* some years ago, and had been fascinated by the expression, 'Sex as the path to super-consciousness.' For her, sex had only brought disappointment. After some dithering, she took a month off from work and travelled to India.

However, the first few days had left her underwhelmed. This place felt more like a private club than a spirituality centre. She had expected to lead a simple, minimalistic life; instead she discovered a tennis court, a swimming pool, a gym and a Jacuzzi. The inmates were desperate for sex, and within forty-eight hours of checking in, a German and a Canadian had tried to hit on her. This place felt like a wild weekend resort in upstate New York.

But Sarah decided she'd give the Ashram a chance. Having spent all that money to get here, she'd try to make the best of it, and hopefully, return with good memories and exotic maroon costumes for her gal pals. And now she had run into this interesting Indian skinhead. This guy could prove to be a useful guide, and she might get to know certain home truths about the Ashram, the HR manager analysed. And yes, she rather liked Thai curry and rice.

It didn't take long for the two to hit it off, and the American was much impressed with the knowledge this man had of her country. His dissection of US politics and the NYC lifestyle was very impressive, more so considering he had never set foot on her soil. Darius used the same trick he had pulled with Naina, and it worked again. Yes, Sarah would really like to see his collection of pictures, and yes, she would definitely like to hear all about his father's experiences at the Ashram.

"I'm leaving tonight. Come meet me in Mumbai when you can. Or, we could go to my hotel, it isn't very far from here. I will show you some interesting heritage sights along the way. And please allow me to pick up the tab; we have to be sweet to our guests. Or you'll return with a poor image of Indian men, and we blokes already have an unflattering one."

Sarah smiled widely. It was three in the afternoon, and this guy would be off in the evening; no harm in taking a quick look. In any case, it had been a rather disappointing journey so far; this might prove to be the interesting distraction she needed. And if this guy tried to act funny, there was always the pepper spray can at her command. She had carried a dozen of those for the India trip.

They hailed an autorickshaw. In a language Sarah didn't comprehend, Darius cheerfully said to the driver: "*Meter mein ghapla nikla toh goti nikaal ke haath mein dalega, bhidu.*"

KAMBLE AND SINGH WERE SIPPING TEA AT A RESTAURANT located near the crime branch office. They had been chatting on the phone, and had decided they should meet up privately to take stock of the situation. Failure had brought the rivals together, and it was time to try and join hands. It also hurt that they had been tasked to work under a retired old man.

Singh was the more agitated of the two, having being compelled to stay put in Mumbai 'until further instructions'.

"I don't understand Khan, sometimes I feel he's gone senile. What the hell is this impotency doctors thing all about? Isn't the killer spewing juice all over the place?"

Kamble sipped his *adrak* tea with extra sugar. The cream biscuits had arrived gratis; the cashier knew who his guests were.

"I have no bloody idea. Khan was a good officer, but his days are over. And this killer is not a fool like Sainath; he won't fall for silly tricks."

"How come the government hasn't asked the CBI to step in? They should have by now, there's so much noise in the media." Singh was secretly hoping the intelligence officers would take over, so he could move on with his life.

"I asked Jasjit sir, he said the Home Minister had given him one last chance after a great deal of persuasion. In any case, the CBI is busy with the coal block scam. These bloody politicians are all thieves."

"Very true. They loot the nation while we chase criminals. But the CBI will have to step in; our teams are going nowhere with this. The DNA sample from Naina's body didn't match with any of the history sheeters, you know." Singh lit a cigarette in the no-smoking joint. The waiter did not object; he just looked away.

"Yes, it's the same story from Bangalore and Goa. In any case, this sounds like the work of a decent, educated man. Our list of history sheeters is mainly roadside criminals. What's your gut feel?"

"I think we are fucked. Worse, my wife has been asking if I am busy having fun in Mumbai's brothels."

Kamble laughed. "I'll take you to a good one very soon. Your missus is already suspecting you, may as well enjoy yourself."

Singh was thrilled. He suddenly began to like this man a bit. The cream biscuits were devoured. Kamble barked at the waiter.

"Raju, do aur packet leke aa! Tabartop!"

AS ONE WOULD EXPECT, SHIT HIT THE CEILING, AND VERY HARD at that. The nation's entire media was on its way to Pune. An American executive's body had been discovered in a down-market lodge located in a down-market area called Swargate. American journalists erroneously termed it 'Sweargate'. This was the kind of lodge where long-distance lorry drivers checked in with hookers they had picked up from the national highway.

It was the same killer. The same chopping off of body parts, the same no-rape-but-semen-on-the-face routine. And this time the instrument of vaginal torture was a cheap liquor bottle, an empty one. Within hours of the first report, the American ambassador to India gate-crashed the Home Minister's office in Delhi, and expressed his anger in no uncertain terms.

"Mister Home Minister, we want the killer identified and caught immediately. We are issuing an alert against travel to India, and this could well become a long-term measure. Please take this matter very seriously. I am told our President is likely to call your Prime Minister later today. And I know you will not like to hear this, but we are happy to fly in an FBI team. They are experienced in tracking serial killers."

Thus insulted, the furious Minister called Jasjit Ahluwalia and expressed great dismay at having put his faith in the crime branch. He banged the phone down without waiting for a response, and called the CBI chief. He ordered him to get cracking on the case. That done, the Minister instructed his office to duck calls from the media.

Khan, accompanied by his team, was already at the scene of the crime. So were the country's finest forensics officers.

Zeenat had been keeping a close eye on the situation, but decided not to disturb her husband. She was half hoping he'd get pulled out of the assignment so they could get on with their peaceful life in Coonoor.

Darius was back in Mumbai. Treating himself and his hash gang to a pitcher at the Alps bar in Colaba, courtesy Jahanbux Irani.

"What's with the new hairdo? You look like a spiritually elevated soul." The men high-fived. Savio was elated to have his usually broke buddy offering to pick up the tab.

"Ah, that's exactly how I feel. In a state of nirvana! Cheers bro!"

A couple of hours later, he got into a brawl with a group of Nigerian men who were chatting rather noisily. After a few punches, realising his little group was out-numbered and out-powered, Darius threatened to file charges against them for drug trafficking, boasting that he knew the local cops. The Nigerian men, swearing loudly, rushed out of Alps.

THIS TIME, KHAN HAD A FACE. THE COPS WERE IN OVERDRIVE, and within an hour, had zeroed in on the suspect. Interrogation with the locals had paid off; the Tibetan vendor confirmed the woman had bought slippers from her shop, and she gave a detailed description of the man who had approached her. She didn't know English terribly well, but had caught the word 'Thai'.

Singh, Kamble and the Pune cops easily located the restaurant. It had no CCTV equipment, but the waiter provided the same description as the slippers seller. And a visit to the German Bakery, which, thanks to the bitter past, had installed surveillance cameras, gave the cops an image. The skinhead's face was on a million television screens, as well as on social media.

The Ashram office gave out details of the victim.

Sarah Fisher, 26, American citizen.

Fingerprints were collected and so were the DNA samples. The lodge owner was promptly arrested; the man claimed he didn't know he was supposed to ask his guests to provide identification. He had never done so in all these years. This statement got him an additional beating inside the police detention room.

Two middle-aged men approached Khan as he was busy studying the blood-soaked room. One of them, who looked like a bank cashier, flashed his CBI card.

"Mr. Azeem Khan, you are off the case, we have taken charge. You can go back home to Coonoor." Jasjit Ahluwalia, who had also arrived, pretended to check the dirty toilet just at that moment. He didn't want to get kicked out in this manner by a couple of officers much younger than him.

A FRANTIC MANHUNT GOT UNDERWAY IN PUNE, EVEN THOUGH the CBI officers suspected the man would have left the city. *Nakabandis* were organised on all roads leading out of the city, including the Mumbai-Pune Expressway.

Jahanbux Irani saw the face on the television set when he had hopped across home for lunch. He disliked eating at the local joints, though he made an exception for his nephew, because Irani didn't wish to invite the bugger home. He froze midway through the mutton *dhansak*. The man on the screen reminded him of someone he had recently met: Darius Irani.

"Oh fuck! Oh fuck! Is it him? It does look like him. It *is* him! What should I do? Should I call that bitch, Jeroo? Should I call the cops? Should I wait? What if I am wrong? How can I report my own nephew? What the fuck? *What the fuck?*"

The old man's brain, usually inactive like a fused bulb from his store, was flushed with thoughts. His wife was in the kitchen making bread pudding. The husband had that dessert for lunch every day, even though the doctor had advised against it. Mrs. Irani did not object beyond a point, for she was a peace-loving woman.

Jeroo did not own a television set, and she did not subscribe to newspapers. And Facebook was out of the question; she hadn't even heard of the damn thing. But the lady from the neighbouring house, whose path she crossed on the way out from home, darted away as soon as she spotted Darius's mother. Jeroo didn't care. She muttered a few cuss words and continued on her way to purchase two eggs and a loaf of bread for dinner.

IT WAS LATE EVENING. SAVIO FRANTICALLY STARTED LOOKING for his hash buddy. He briskly scanned the lanes of Colaba with no luck. He even dared to ring the doorbell, but was spared abuse because Jeroo wasn't at home. At last he spotted Darius enjoying a beer at Leopold's, as he regaled a couple of back-packers with his on-the-tap humour.

"Boss, we need to talk."

"Guys, meet Savio, my best bud. The coolest human being in the world. Savio, come join us, Adam and Mark are buying us beers tonight."

"Listen, it's urgent. Come out. NOW."

Reluctantly, Darius stepped out. Savio grabbed his arm and dragged him to a lonely back-lane.

"Man, the serial killer looks just like you. Were you in Pune yesterday?"

"Balls. I was chilling at home all day, and then I met you guys at Alps, remember?" He then burst into loud laughter. "Fucker, what did you smoke today? Rolled coke in your joint?" More laughter.

Savio, while hunting for his friend, had already recalled that Darius was in Bangalore at the time of the techie's murder. But he did not share this thought with Darius, partly because he was in a state of panic, and partly because of the fear he always harboured of his volatile buddy. Savio only managed to say, "Listen, be careful. The cops will catch you, taking you to be the killer. He looks just like you."

Darius shooed him away, but quickly wore his glares. He hurried to join Adam and Mark for the beers. He wasn't going to let go of free booze because of alarmist Savio. He also managed to borrow a thousand bucks from his newly-formed friends.

"Guys, mom's not too well, I badly need some dosh." For the Aussie back-packers, it was no big deal; they were happy to help. And they just had fun with an Indian, the first time since they had arrived in India a couple of weeks before.

After the good-byes, Darius decided to disappear for a few days. "The chase begins now in true earnest," he smiled to himself. He headed straight for CST Station. Unknown to him, Mumbai cops were already on the lookout at all major railway stations.

KHAN AND AHLUWALIA QUIETLY SLIPPED OUT FROM THE CRIME scene, and drove to the German Bakery for a cup of tea. Koregaon Park was buzzing more than usual because news of the killing of an Ashram inmate had got the locals excited. The place was packed. Ahluwalia got a young couple ejected from the corner table.

"So that's it, Jasjit! Guess it's time for me to return to farming."

"No, Khan, hold on for a while. Let the CBI guys do their number, we'll continue with our investigations. We have a headstart over these guys, and now we have the bloody criminal's face."

"Well Jasjit, you can handle it from here. Let me go."

"No, don't give up just yet, not after all the hard work. You are not a quitter, Khan. I know that. And it's now become a question of the crime branch's reputation."

Secretly, Khan was hoping to hear those words from his ex-colleague. Yes, he was no quitter; he hated losing. Yes, he had retired from service; yes, he did not want to be a part of this mess, but having agreed to work on the case, he knew he wouldn't be able to live with himself if he gave up at this stage. Khan lit a cigarette. A waiter promptly arrived to point to the No Smoking sign. Ahluwalia dismissed him from sight without even bothering to look at the man's face.

"Okay, let's get this bastard. Dead or alive." Khan, having taken in deep drags, stubbed the cigarette on the floor. His eyes were blazing, he was breathing heavily. Khan called Zeenat, and without saying hello, barked that she should not call him for some days.

"Whatever the hell happens." And he walked off without saying a word to his companion.

Ahluwalia smiled. This was the Khan of the past. Angry, determined, focused. This was the Khan he had been waiting patiently to see again.

He hadn't forgotten how Khan had dealt with that juvenile rapist all those years ago.

A 16-YEAR-OLD LAD HAD BEEN SENT TO THE JUVENILE JUSTICE Home for reformation after he had been convicted for taking part in a gangrape. Khan, who had led the investigation, was not amused with the verdict, and he believed that adolescents involved in felony crimes must be considered as adults.

One day, two years into his reform procedure, the juvenile, now an 18-year-old, had been found stabbed to death inside his isolation room. Sachin Wagh had not been allowed to mingle with other inmates for fear that he could be attacked, as it often happens with rape convicts. Investigations into how a knife had reached the Juvenile Justice Home had led nowhere. There were murmurs in a section of the police force that an insider was involved. The media had picked up the story, but the mysterious stabbing was forgotten after a couple of days, as a new financial scam hit the headlines.

It was the handiwork of a young, hot-blooded Khan. The warden was his old friend; the two had played street cricket as kids. Khan was smuggled into the premises late at night, and the rapist's door had been left unlocked. He shoved a pillow over the convict's face, and pierced the knife through his heart. And then spat on the bloodied corpse. The news brought a great deal of joy to the public and there was jubilation in the streets.

Some months later, on a night patrol, Khan boasted about his deed to Jasjit Ahluwalia. The latter was immensely proud of his colleague, and bought him a bottle of Black & White Scotch whisky. Ahluwalia shared Khan's ideology: If the State is unable to deliver justice, it must be meted out offline. Ahluwalia had been involved in numerous fake encounters, and had planned one for Sachin Wagh as soon as he was to be set free. But Khan had beaten him to it.

TAKEN OFF THE CASE, KAMBLE AND SINGH DROVE TO MUMBAI together. Singh was delighted his days in the city were done. It was time to return home, where great food waited. But he hadn't forgotten Kamble's delicious offer, and decided it was time to take him up on it. And his temporary pal was only too happy to help. They went straight to Foras Road, brothel number 227. Kamble's favourite was Mala, a Nepali prostitute, always much in demand. Not only did she have a pleasant, happy face, a rare thing for Foras Road, but she was a blow job expert. And because Kamble was a senior cop, Mala would put her heart and soul into the task.

Tonight he decided his partner-in-failure should enjoy the 227 speciality, and picked another prostitute for himself. As Mala and Singh walked into a dingy room, Kamble shouted out to her, "Be good to him, my friend is going through a rough time."

Mala smiled, and ordered two beers be promptly dispatched to the room. This was going to be a drain on the brothel's resources, but the madam didn't mind. You keep cops happy, you remain happy. That's one mantra all the owners of whorehouses in Mumbai never forget.

After Mala did her number, which didn't take much time because the officer had been starved of sex, Singh decided it was time for beer and talk. He liked to chat up prostitutes after he had been taken care of; it was more fun spending time with them than the perpetually crabby Mrs. Singh. That moron didn't even know how to please him in bed. Mala casually enquired if any progress had been made in the serial killing case, though she didn't know Singh was one of the officers in hot pursuit. The murderer's gruesome deeds had got the brothel inmates pretty worried. The girls were used to sadistic customers, but this one was way beyond it.

"We'll catch that *behenchod* soon."

"Sahib, we saw the man's picture on TV. Someone who looks quite like him had come to visit number 37 some months ago. My friend Vidya told me. You should speak to her."

Singh sat up on the metal bed, it creaked under his weight. "Really? What did she say?"

"She said he was a crazy guy. That he tried his best, but failed to have sex. There must be something wrong with him." Mala shook her head, as she put on her blouse. "We do land up with such impotent types now and then. It's quite frustrating; they waste our time, leave unhappy, and don't bother to tip us."

Khan's words started ringing in his ears.

"Get teams in Bangalore, Delhi and Goa cracking on the local doctors who deal with impotency issues."

He quickly zipped up, gulped down the beer in one go, dropped a hundred rupee note on the bed, and rushed out of number 227.

DARIUS STOOD STARING AT THE DEPARTURES INDICATOR. HE randomly picked the Howrah Mail, and then did something unusual; he stood in the queue to buy a ticket. Train journeys were always ticketless; you either bribed or threatened the ticket checker into submission. That's how Darius always travelled. But tonight he didn't want unnecessary distractions; he needed to be invisible for a while.

However, as soon as he boarded the train, he was spotted by a cop in plain clothes. The constable followed Darius into the bogie, and occupied a seat a little distance away. But the man did not act. Dinner was eaten, and the passengers gradually retired into their allocated berths. Darius was perched on the top one. He wasn't sleeping; he was thinking.

"The second stage of my work has begun," he smiled to himself. "Real fun will start only now." But that's for later; he first needed to get his wallet fattened. "That is top priority, man."

At about 2 a.m., Darius felt a gentle tap on his shoulder. A middle-aged man softly whispered into his ear. "Police. Don't worry, I just want to ask you a few questions. Get down very quietly and join me near the door."

It was an alert cop. Even though Darius was wearing a cap, he could notice the close resemblance to India's Most Wanted Man. But he had to be sure, and the desire to be a hero prevented him from passing on the discovery to the control room. A fatal error.

They were standing by the closed train door. The cop demanded to know the suspect's identity. Darius quickly looked around; there was no one. Ordinarily he would have liked to have a fun exchange with the chap and later pick his pocket. It brought Darius great joy to steal from policemen. But there was no time to lose tonight. In one swift action, he yanked open the door of the Howrah Mail's general class compartment, and pushed the cop out. It was all over in a flash. And it wasn't really the constable's fault; he might have expected some trouble, but he wasn't prepared for a lightning death strike.

No one heard a thing as most of the passengers were fast asleep. Darius decided to enjoy the cool breeze. He stood half outside the door and let the wind hit his face. He had been sick to the core of the pyjama-clad fat old man sleeping right below him, as the man had been continuously farting all the crap he had consumed for dinner. Darius took in deep breaths, shut the door tight, and returned to his berth. On his way up, he kicked the farter, who woke up with a start.

"Sorry uncle, I missed a step. Am not well and have loose motions. In fact, I crapped a little on my berth."

The farter stopped farting, and nervously alighted to look for a vacant berth elsewhere on the train. Darius decided to chill for a bit. The next move would have to happen very soon.

KHAN WAS IN THE POLICE CAR, SMOKING AND PONDERING ON his next course of action. He thought of calling Zeenat to apologise for his rude conduct, but decided against it. He reminded himself that he must focus all his attention on the bloody killer. The swine was winning this war.

Although 9.30 p.m. is considered late by Pune standards, Khan decided to visit the popular joints to check if the suspect had been spotted. Gut-feel told him it was unlikely the man belonged to Pune. The lethal behaviour, the give-a-damn attitude, and the skill to nail smart young women indicated traits of a big city slicker. He instructed the driver to first get to MG Road, the street a tourist or an outsider is most likely to drop by, aside from the happening Koregaon Park. It was a shot in the dark, but one worth taking for a retired cop who had just been sacked.

Khan tried to gather information from some of the restaurants in the area, but no one reported having seen the suspect. He then asked the driver to turn to Moledina Road, and considered the SGS Mall located to the right. He then remembered Coffee House, which was located on his side of the road. Khan had been to the place a few times. His luck finally turned.

The waiters were confident the man had indeed been there for lunch, accompanied by an old Parsi gentleman. One of the waiters had observed him carefully, and had quietly sniggered when the chap dropped a dollop of gunpowder into the already spicy *sambhar*, and had then begun crying like a baby.

Pune's small city life had paid off for Khan. This breakthrough would have been almost impossible to achieve in a big city. The cashier said he knew the old gent. Quite well, in fact.

"Sir, he runs a lampshades store on MG Road. Very nice man."

Just then an excited Singh called. "The killer had been to Foras Road. I spoke to a prostitute called Vidya, who says it must be the same man. And you were right, sir. The man can't get it up."

Kamble, who was standing next to him, was pissed off to hear the word 'I'.

"Shouldn't this bastard have said 'We'? It was I who got him the special Mala blow job." But he decided to keep quiet.

"I will deal with this cunt at the right time," he reassured himself.

"Good work. Hope you had fun at Foras Road. Both of you meet me at my office tomorrow noon. I think we've got the son of a bitch."

"Er, sir, I had gone there only on work. But what about the CBI?"

"Screw them. Let them do what the fuck they want. Our plan remains unchanged." Khan smiled just a little bit. For the first time since he had left the tranquility of the Nilgiris.

JAHANBUX IRANI WAS ABOUT TO OPEN HIS SHOP. HE HAD arrived late that day, and the attendant, the only one he had cared to hire, stared at him accusingly for making her wait. Usually she would get a mouthful for arriving five minutes late, and today Hitler was an hour behind schedule. She wanted to wring his old neck, but quickly swallowed her annoyance, being the sole earning member of a large family. However shitty this job, it was much needed.

Renuka didn't know Irani hadn't slept a wink the previous night. He had been riding on the horns of a great dilemma. But his internal morality debate ended as soon as the shop shutter clanked open. A police car screeched to a halt right behind the retailer. Khan, accompanied by two Pune cops, emerged and without saying a word, whisked the man into the vehicle.

Even as Irani started protesting rather loudly, inviting unneeded attention on the busy MG Road, Khan turned to the puzzled but amused attendant.

"Police. Boss is coming with us to Mumbai. You will have to manage the store for some days."

The young woman looked thrilled at the prospect.

The journey to Mumbai did not include a halt, not even a loo break. This had turned the short-tempered man edgy. Irani knew what this was about. He knew this was trouble, and the tension had further weakened his old bladder. The passenger kept shouting questions, but there was no response from the cops. Not a word.

As soon as they reached Navi Mumbai, Khan turned around to face him. "Mr. Irani, don't worry, you aren't in trouble. We just want to know who you had lunch with the day before yesterday."

The uncle fell silent. The morality debate began haunting him all over again. Jahanbux Irani involuntarily peed inside the dusty Qualis.

KHAN HAD THE MURDERER'S IDENTITY, THE TABLES HAD finally turned. The lampshades seller spilled the beans faster than Khan had expected, and this meant the case was pretty much solved. All that the CBI chaps had to do now was track down the culprit. But Khan wasn't going to share the information, not just yet. He knew from past experience that they would hog all the credit, and he would be left with not even a thank you note after all the hard work and stress.

After the interrogation was done, Khan considered letting Irani go, as he figured the man had nothing to do with the murders. It was clear Darius needed the money, and that was why he hit on his uncle. The three-hour-long discussion told Khan that the man had maintained very little contact with his dead brother's family in Mumbai. All the same, Irani was detained, 'just in case some additional information is required', he was told. The real reason was Khan didn't want this guy on the loose; he looked like a businessman whose tongue moved faster than his lampshades.

Soon after, the core team met. Kamble and Singh watched him intently. Khan looked rather pleased with himself, and this was a good sign.

"Keep it strictly confidential. The killer's name is Darius Irani. He lives in Colaba."

Kamble jumped from his seat. "Great! Let's go nab him!"

Khan raised his hand. "It won't be so easy, he must have already left the city. He's not stupid, you know. Darius lives with his aged mother, and there's no one else in the family. I'm off to meet her now. What you gentlemen do is immediately contact your Colaba *khabris* for dope on this guy. I want as much information as possible."

Singh looked a bit confused. "How did you crack this case, sir?"

"All that for later. Let's get the killer first."

"But we've been taken off the investigation. Shouldn't we share this information with the CBI and let them handle it?" Singh didn't want any further role to play in this madness. He had already planned a few quick visits to Mala before flying off into the arms of his nagging missus.

Khan reacted with anger, something his assistants had not experienced before. "No. This is my case and I will deal with it. No one will say a word to the CBI. If you don't obey this order, I will ensure both of you are instantly transferred to a Naxal area, and that's a bloody promise."

The two officers left without uttering another word. Khan called Zeenat.

"Only a few more days, then I am done. Things are looking good."

She smiled. Mrs. Khan recognised the tone of his voice. It meant Khan was in a good mood. "Take care of yourself and I hope you have been taking your blood pressure pills regularly."

He hadn't. He had switched to cigarettes. And drinking. And thinking of Shraddha. But she wasn't told that.

KHAN WALKED INTO THE OLD, DILAPIDATED BUILDING. HE could see that the structure was in urgent need of repairs. He smiled at a few residents he met along the way to avoid suspicion. This must appear like a social call.

A tired old woman opened the door. She looked rather annoyed.

"Who the hell are you? What the hell do you want? Are you here to sell me something? If so, I shall call the police and get you arrested. Get out!"

Khan was just a little bit flustered. He wasn't used to anyone talking to him in that manner. He felt an urgent temptation to pull the old hag by her thinning gray hair. "Bitch, how did you raise your son?" Instead, he shoved one foot inside, so that the door wouldn't slam on him.

"Relax, my dear lady. I am a policeman. I want to have a word with you."

Jeroo Irani took a step back, and the arthritic pain shot through both her knees. She knew this had to do with Darius. She had always dreaded this day would come.

The uninvited guest gently stepped inside and shut the door behind him. "Ma'am, this is serious. It's in your interest to keep things calm, else your neighbours will get involved, and that won't do you any good."

Jeroo, walking like a zombie, fell on the dusty sofa. Khan avoided sitting next to her; he went and stood by the window sill. Then came those words, words that Jeroo had feared she would hear one day.

"We believe your son has hurt a few people. We need to talk to him. Where can I find him?"

Jeroo's throat had gone dry, she went blank. Khan offered to fetch water, but she did not respond. There was silence for a minute. Then she spoke, without looking at her guest.

"Did he kill anyone?"

"Right now he's only needed for questioning, and we need your help. Where can we find him?" Khan said this even as he realised the poor woman was unlikely to know. He could sense this was a dysfunctional family.

"I don't know, Darius hasn't been home in days."

"Does he carry a cell phone?" Khan knew the answer but the question had to be asked.

"No."

"Think he may have gone to a relative's place?"

"No."

"Who else lives in this house?"

"Only the two of us. He is my only child, his father passed away around twenty years ago." Jeroo broke down. "Officer, please tell me the truth. Is Darius in trouble?"

Khan felt a sudden pity for this old woman. She was paying the price for an out-of-control son.

"Well, let me just say this – he will be in trouble if he doesn't contact me quickly. Mrs. Irani, will you call me as soon as he's back? This is for your son's own good."

He dropped a card next to her. Jeroo didn't bother to look at it, as she was staring emptily at the floor.

"One last thing. Do you have his picture? Recent one?"

"No. I only have pictures from his childhood days, when his father was alive. Why did my husband leave me so soon, why am I alive?" Now she had begun to sob.

Khan tapped her on the shoulder. "Take care of yourself, Mrs. Irani."

As he walked out of the building, he lit a cigarette and called Kamble. "Am texting you the address. Immediately post a few constables in plain clothes. I want them here 24x7."

ON RECEIVING A CALL FROM KHAN, AHLUWALIA BARKED orders to have the entire Colaba area put under surveillance. Informers had already started sending in reports. Yes, they had seen this chap hanging around on the streets; yes, he had the habit of getting into quarrels; and yes, he had often been spotted doing drugs.

Even as the crime branch chief pulled at his large moustache in triumph, he realised protocol demanded he call the chief of CBI and provide all the information gathered so far.

He rolled the glass paperweight on his desk, and began to think. No. Khan and his boys had done all the hard work, and he couldn't let outsiders cheat them out of their glory. In any case, the suspect was still on the run, so that needed to be dealt with first. Ahluwalia concluded the best thing to do was keep things quiet for now. And if questioned later, he could always say they were tracking a suspect involved in another crime, and that the serial killer fell into their lap. But he knew the CBI chief Ramesh Iyengar wasn't an idiot, and he'd know his command had been disobeyed.

"Ass needs to be covered, Jasjit. Think man, think."

After a few more minutes of paperweight spinning, he made up his mind. He called Iyengar on the hotline, and came to the point only after a few pleasantries had been exchanged. Ahluwalia knew he must not sound excited, that would be a dead giveaway.

"Mr. Iyengar, my team has worked really hard on the case. Is it okay with you if we carry on with our parallel investigations? Of course, we'll let you know if something significant comes up."

"Hmm. Jasjit, the Minister's clear orders are to keep you guys away, and he sounds really upset with you in particular. How will you deal with that?"

"Don't worry. If questioned, I'll handle it."

"Okay, so then he's your problem, not mine. Also make sure your boys keep away from mine. Don't want a battle of egos."

"Done!"

Both asses covered. Time to move on.

IT WAS ABOUT 4 A.M. A STATION WAS APPROACHING, AND Darius saw a few passengers heading towards the door. He quietly slipped down from his berth, and took a little walk around. He spotted a middle-aged woman fast asleep, a handbag stuck under her armpit. He waited for the station to arrive. As soon as it did, he carefully dug out the bag, and slipped out onto the platform.

He read the station's name. Bhusaval. Down-market. Just what the doctor might order, Darius smiled. He began to exit, and asked a couple of fellow passengers disembarking from the train if they knew of a lodge nearby. He was told he'd find a few just down the road. Once outside the station, Darius stopped to check the contents of the bag. Apart from the usual ladies thingies, he found twenty thousand rupees. It was time to celebrate; he had hit on the right target. Darius broke into a little jig, much to the amusement of sleepy passengers walking behind him.

Hotel Yatri Niwas. "Perfect. Check in, catch up on some sleep. And then plan for some action."

Darius had to kick the smelly reception desk repeatedly to get attention. One very sleepy little boy grudgingly arrived. He asked him to come after 8 a.m., 'when the staff arrives'. Darius slipped a hundred-buck note into his little shirt pocket. This gesture immediately woke the Bhusaval lad.

"Where will I go at this time of the night? Hero, give me a vacant room, and I will check in when your people arrive. Be a good boy now."

And so he got a room to himself. The bedsheet was unwashed, he spotted stains and strands of human hair, but these minor issues had never mattered to Darius. His mom wouldn't do the laundry for weeks, and even when she did, it was with a pinchful of cheap detergent powder. The idea was to crash for as long as possible and then figure the way forward.

KAMBLE, SINGH AND TEAM HAD BEEN INSTRUCTED TO COLLECT more information on Darius. "Track down his friends, speak with the neighbours and locals at Colaba. Someone may have a clue on where he has gone; perhaps he has a hideout."

Singh had suggested alerting all the international airports in case Darius decided to flee the nation, but Khan shot the idea down. Instinct told him this man had no passport, so there was no need to even talk to the passport authorities, leave alone create an airport alarm. One thing Khan had realised after meeting Jeroo was that the killer was using basic tools to outwit the nation's cops. And this fact hurt the most. It was one thing to be outsmarted by a tech-savvy geek, quite another being made to look like fools by a common criminal. Intelligent yes, but still a bloody common criminal.

Khan was back in the saddle, staring at the soft board. He needed to make some quick observations, now that he'd identified the culprit. Ahluwalia walked in.

"Khan, not very good news. I'm told the CBI's sleuths have managed to track down this fucker; apparently they got a lead from some Nigerian drug pushers who are already in police custody. In fact, they are meeting his mother today."

"Well, that's fine, actually. It takes the guilt away from us, of withholding information."

"But the mother will tell them she has already spoken to you."

"Doubtful. She's messed up in the head, and I didn't leave a name behind." Khan lied to get Ahluwalia off his back. He had more important matters on hand.

"You better be right, Khan. I certainly don't want that old moron they've chosen as Home Minister calling again. By the way, what's the next plan?"

"We are at it, Jasjit. I have to draw this guy's character sketch more carefully. We have to try and predict his next move, that's our best bet. We can't out-run this man, we have to out-think him."

Ahluwalia didn't say a word. He wasn't a believer in such hocus pocus; he believed in instant action and instant justice. But past experience told him that sometimes Khan's methods did pay off, so it was best to leave him alone. But before leaving, he couldn't resist a snigger.

"One good thing is, the next time this *madarchod* strikes, the blame will be on the CBI, not us."

KHAN HUNG A PRINT OF THE SUSPECT'S CCTV GRAB ON THE board, and began to make fresh observations.

Hard object used to smash the victim's head.
Seeks instant death, does not want to torture the victims. Could also be trying to avoid anyone hearing screams.
He's physically strong. Need to keep this in mind in case of a face-off. Must keep the gun loaded, can't match this guy in brute power.
No rape, but strange objects being used for penetration.
Sadistic tendency. Is he religious? Is this some sort of a pagan ritual? What's the point of this?
He's got a sexual problem. Prostitute Vidya has confirmed this. He also deeply hates women. Is Jeroo Irani responsible for this? Need to spend quality time with her to learn about her son's past.
Limbs chopped off.

More sadism. Women hater.

Again, he's mind-fucked. Need to meet Jeroo. And also Jahanbux; maybe he knows something.

Ejaculation on the face, before or after death.

Very odd. The ladies weren't rejecting him, they appeared to be happy to be with him. Perhaps another sign of women hating.

Young women, all in their twenties.

This could be because he is an attractive man, and finds dating easier with young women. He needs to win their confidence so that they agree to meet him in private places.

Smart bugger, he's picking the victims carefully. A lady charmer, and this is the most dangerous part of all.

Different cities.

Is he trying to escape being seen/caught? Or is he trying to prove a point? Perhaps he wants national recognition, most serial killers seek recognition.

He's having a blast. He wants a big bang for his buck. This could also mean the killer knows he'll eventually go down, and he wants to do the 9/11 equivalent of sexual violence. Don't think he's going to stop now.

Killer is a Luddite. Perhaps.

A tech challenged sort. Or, smart enough not to use the cell phone for his murderous deeds.

Yes, he's screwing us with common tricks. Bastard. No tech means we have to use old-fashioned investigative methods.

Tall, powerfully built, perhaps in his late twenties/early thirties.

We are dealing with a tough nut. Murders must be easy to execute.

White collared, perhaps a corporate executive or a businessman.
Bad news. The culprit is intelligent, this is no fool like Sainath. We are in trouble.
An unemployed intelligent man. Lethal combination. He has nothing to lose, has no family of his own. Jeroo doesn't count, she's too old.
Killing for pleasure, not money.
More bad news. He's begun to have a blast; there is no clear motive, and he will strike again. VERY SOON.
Yes, he will.

Khan lit a cigarette. He tried to form a rough description in his head. "An educated lunatic on the loose, looking for recognition through a murderous orgy, hates women because they are not able to sexually satisfy him, is smart enough to be able to evade arrest for so long, has a fucked-up past, mental sickness or childhood abuse indicated."

He called his crime branch contacts in Chennai and Kolkata, and asked them to keep a lookout for the suspect at railway stations and bus stops. It was clear the murderer was on *Bharat Darshan*, and that he favoured big city women.

Just then a constable arrived. "Sahib, a woman has come to meet you, she insists she knows you very well. Should I throw her out, she looks like a, er, slum dweller."

Khan, lost in thought, continued staring at the soft board. "What does she want?"

"Sahib, I don't know. She says she'll only speak to you."

"What's her name?"

"Shraddha."

A rush of emotion flooded Khan's face. It was the expression of a lover who's suddenly run into his long lost love. Wisely, he didn't turn around to look at the constable.

"Okay, send her in."

"But sahib, she looks like a…"

"Send her in."

AN EXCITED *KHABRI* CALLED KAMBLE.

"Sir, this fellow is a drug addict."

"So what? Give me some hard leads."

"I have seen him smoke hashish near Horniman Circle. He has a regular gang."

"Do you know who these people are?"

"Not really sir, but one of them is a Colaba boy. I've seen him around."

"Okay, I'm reaching there now; show me the place."

Kamble and a few constables reached the spot, and he ordered one of them to be stationed there every evening, and to immediately call if the hash gang was spotted.

As luck would have it, the group arrived that evening itself, minus Darius Irani. Kamble rushed to pick them up for questioning. They were formally charged with drug possession and possible trafficking, and this helped keep them in custody for days together.

But it didn't take long for Savio to break down. He was a simple man who liked the odd smoke, and the hilarious Darius was the ideal companion on a hash trip. Savio didn't want to be a part of this mess; he had four unmarried sisters to worry about, and his brother was unemployed at the age of 25. He spilled the beans, and spoke about the Bangalore trip. Kamble was excited.

"You have the wedding pictures?"

"Yes sir, at home."

"Great. Give me all of them, and I shall drop the drug trafficking charge against you and your pals."

The crime branch team had the culprit's latest photographs, so things should become easy from now, Kamble thought. He rushed to meet Khan, without bothering to inform Sushant Singh.

AS SOON AS SHRADDHA WALKED IN, LONG EXTINGUISHED feelings were rekindled, but the man didn't show it. Khan coldly asked her to meet him in the evening at a bar near Santacruz railway station. He would have liked to spend quality time with her right there in the make-shift office, but did not want the staff to start gossiping. Already the constable's tone of voice had alarmed Khan.

That evening, Shraddha spoke at length about her life, and Khan was filled with sadness. But he was also happy that she wasn't dead. He held her hand, and promised financial help. The woman was overwhelmed, and broke down. More than the money, it had to do with his gentle touch; it was the balm she had been craving all these years, a balm on a soul that had been repeatedly battered and abused.

As he took her back home in a cab, Shraddha hesitatingly offered to go to the hotel where they would often meet in the past. Khan immediately took up her offer, for Zeenat was nowhere on his mind tonight. Shraddha had always satisfied him; she knew what to do and where and when. Zeenat had been a dud in bed; a cold, passive partner. A perfect wife, but an awful sex mate.

They made passionate love. Many times. Khan lit a cigarette, happy to discover he still had it in him. The ageing man had long forgotten what mating was all about. But this was Shraddha, Magic Shraddha. The woman who knew what to do and where and when. Suhas had not been fortunate to see this side of his wife. For him, sex was equal to rape. Unless the partner howled in pain, there was no point in it.

As he licked her hands, Shraddha asked about the serial killer.

"Sahib, how's it going? Any progress? I saw you on television, you looked worried."

"It's work in progress, we'll nab him soon."

"He has a mother, right? Why don't you put her on television? She can plead with him to return home, she can say she is very unwell. Sons usually listen to mothers."

This was another reason why Khan adored this woman. She was uneducated, she was poor, but she had a brain with ideas. Earthy ideas that worked out there. He knew the ploy was unlikely to work with the hardened Darius, but there was no harm trying.

Khan made love to her one more time. This time he went down on her. Shraddha dearly wished the night would never end. This was a novel experience for her. Khan later slipped a thick bundle of rupee notes into her purse.

AN URGENT MEETING WAS CALLED AT THE CRIME BRANCH office board room and everyone appeared excited, except for Jasjit Ahluwalia.

"Officers, Iyengar has come to know we are concealing information, and he isn't very happy about it."

Ignoring him, an impatient Kamble triumphantly rose from his chair. "Sir, I have the killer's latest pictures!" He circulated prints from Savio's album. "We have to put these out in the media."

Singh stared at him, but said nothing. He had seen such a thing coming.

Khan patted him on the back. "Good work, Kamble. Also, I have a suggestion. We have to put Jeroo Irani on air, she's a good bet."

All of them turned to the crime branch boss who didn't look very impressed. "All very fine, but what the hell should we do about the CBI? The case has been officially transferred to them. Officially, people."

Khan thought for a moment. "Let's share our findings with them and get out of the picture. There's no other option."

"But Khan, your team has been doing good work! Okay, I'll speak to them and request special permission for you to continue the investigation, with a clear understanding that you will keep the CBI updated on a daily basis. Is that okay?"

The three appeared to have no objection to this, not that they said anything. Ahluwalia called Iyengar and put up the proposal. To his surprise, the latter was open to the idea.

"You know, Jasjit, I have great regard for Azeem. He was a good officer. I don't mind him working independently."

Ahluwalia heaved a sigh of relief as he did not like to give up control easily. He mailed Darius's pictures to Iyengar, and in return, the CBI agreed to the suggestion that Mrs. Irani publicly address her son.

"Ask Azeem to convince Jeroo. He can also sit beside her in the TV studio. I'm told he was the first to meet her, and she has been asking for him. I think the old lady likes him."

Iyengar killed two birds with a single stroke. From the time he was appointed chief of the intelligence agency a year ago, he had been keen to change the popular perception of the CBI. He didn't like the organisation's 'arrogant guys' image. Iyengar also made sure he had the services of Khan available to him. His team had made little progress so far, and the Home Minister had been tormenting him with regular phone calls.

KHAN INVITED JEROO FOR LUNCH TO THE GOLDEN DRAGON AT the Taj Mahal Hotel. This was a ploy to soften the lady. He had seen the dump Irani was living in. Khan had also realised the woman was crazy, and perhaps she'd be more civilised in a place like this.

The depressed and frightened Jeroo readily agreed. She knew her son was going down, and there was nothing she could do about it, except curse her loser of a husband. This old officer who had dropped by her home seemed like a gentleman, and a free lunch at the Taj would be nice, thank you. The wretched Ronnie had never been able to pamper her. Jeroo's entire life had gone walking past the super luxury hotel, wondering what went on inside.

"Mrs. Irani, we need your help."

"I have already told you I have no idea where my son is. He can't even call me as we don't have a telephone. We can't afford one." She stabbed the Wok Braised Lamb Shank, 'delicately cooked in tangy ginger oyster sauce', as the waiter had pointed out, even as he wondered what this hag was doing in a place like this. Or so Jeroo thought.

"Yes ma'am, I'm aware of that. That's why we want you to go on television and make an appeal to him."

For a moment the thought of being seen on television excited the woman. That would score her brownie points with the neighbours. But she quickly retreated into her negativity mode.

"No use, man. He gives a shit about what I think and feel. The bastard."

The last word was uttered a bit too loudly, causing a few awkward glances being thrown in their direction. One does not utter cuss words inside the Taj. It's an unwritten rule, though it was broken during the 26/11 terror attack. Clearly the Dragon had done little to inspire civility in this frustrated old lady. Khan decided to keep the conversation going.

"It's a chance we have to take. We don't know where your son has run off to, and we fear he may harm someone else. We need your cooperation."

"It's a waste of time. Tell me, when you find him, will you shoot him dead?"

The unexpected question briefly surprised Khan, but he didn't show it. He had come prepared; this insane woman was capable of anything.

"No way, ma'am. Rest assured the police want him alive."

All of a sudden, she started weeping into her lamb. "Darius is all I have, officer. Promise me you won't harm him. I have nothing left in this world, he is everything to me. He's a good boy, a victim of circumstance, that's all."

He gently touched her palm which felt rough, like that of a factory worker.

"This woman has slogged all her life." Khan felt a little sorry for her. He also felt bad because he had lied. Khan had already made up his mind: When he'd eventually meet the monster, his first action would be to shoot at his balls.

He decided to stay quiet for a bit, allowing time for this unfortunate woman to recover her composure. Khan didn't really mind her swearing inside the la-di-dah joint, but her sobbing was much too embarrassing.

And then came the sudden change of heart. "Okay, I'll do it. I trust you. But can you help me a little in return? Please?"

"Sure, anything we can do."

"I need a new fridge. Mine is thirty years old and it's nearly dead. Surely you people can do this much for an old woman who may never see her only son again."

Khan was relieved. He was worried she would ask for some sort of legal concessions for her son, and that would be impossible to promise. "Consider it done. A brand new refrigerator will reach you this evening."

"Thank you so much, officer, and a frost-free one please." Jeroo's tears had evaporated, and Khan decided he'd slip in a tricky question.

"Mrs. Irani, I hope you don't mind me asking a silly question. It's my job to ask such questions, and so I must. Just wondering if you have any idea that your son might be impotent?"

Jeroo froze in her seat, as if struck by lightning. She didn't say a word, only stared at the ceiling for a few minutes.

She later said, "I don't know." And then went on to finish her meal.

"Would you like anything for dessert, ma'am?" The snooty waiter was back. Jeroo wanted to slap his rotund face and she rudely demanded to see the menu card. Her choice was immediate, much to Khan's surprise.

"Seasonal Fruit Flambé. Now scoot you fool, I'm in an important meeting."

Khan turned his face away so that Jeroo would not catch his smile. He felt like laughing out loud. Not just because this poor woman had chosen the most expensive dessert, the only yardstick she had apparently used; the look on the waiter's face was to die for. No one would have spoken to him like that at the Golden Dragon. Not even the 26/11 terrorists.

IYENGAR DECREED THAT A SENIOR CBI OFFICER WOULD address the press conference, and that Khan would sit silently next to the suspect's mother.

The room was, as expected, packed to the gills. There were camera crews and reporters in every nook and cranny. Jeroo Irani, dressed in a sky blue sari, the only one she owned, and one she hadn't worn in twenty years, was seated in the centre. On one side was Azeem Khan, and on the other, the CBI man.

The room went into a frenzy when Darius's wedding album pictures were projected on a large screen. After the pointless question and answer session was done, Mrs. Irani was asked to address her son. Khan gave her a reassuring look, a gentle tap on the shoulder, as she turned to him for moral support. She then began to read out from a handwritten statement which Khan had helped her prepare.

"Darius, my dearest son, please come home. I have been very unwell. The police won't harm you; they only want to speak with you. I know you are not to blame for all that's happened, the world has been bad to you. Even the police knows that. Come home, please, your mother needs you, I beg of you." She then coughed for effect, and grabbed the glass of apple juice that had been laid out for her.

This brought the conference to a close, but one smarty-pants journalist shouted out a question to the silent Khan.

"Mr. Azeem Khan, are you still investigating the case? We were told you had been sacked after the CBI took over."

Khan wanted to grab a pistol and shoot at the pest's big mouth. He hesitatingly moved closer to the microphone and said, "I am only helping out in whatever way I can. I have retired from active service."

And then he helped Jeroo walk out of the room, as the whirring cameras caught their every movement. Zeenat was watching the live show. She was livid at the public humiliation of her husband. "I must have a word with Khan. This nonsense has to stop."

"KHAN, GET BACK HOME, IT'S NOT WORTH IT." HER TEXT message read.

It suddenly occurred to Khan that he hadn't spoken to his wife in days. He must call, and he must remain careful with his tone of voice. Shraddha was very much back in his life, and the very sharp Zeenat would sense it. He decided to play safe, opting for the SMS route.

"Will be back soon, we are on the verge of catching this killer. How are you?"

Even as he was slowly typing the words, his mind raced to the past, when an anonymous caller had informed Zeenat about his liaison with a prostitute. Khan had not bothered to find out who it was, though he suspected a colleague who had been the jealous sort. Khan had played dirty politics and engineered the rat's transfer to the unhappening Akola, which he knew would kill the man's mighty ego. It not only killed that, it killed his soul too and the cop was found hanging from the ceiling fan one evening, inside the police station.

But Zeenat hadn't let the incident die down easily; the phone call had driven a wedge in their otherwise happy marriage. It had taken a couple of years and a thousand reassurances for Zeenat to quit discussing the phone call, but things were never the same again. They never are when trust breaks down in a relationship. She still loved him deeply, but the scar never healed.

And to think Khan was back in Shraddha's arms. He felt guilty, but this prostitute brought solace to him. She was like a drug he found hard to resist. Yes, he was planning to use the drug a few more times while he was in Mumbai, and no, Zeenat would not know about it. He was retired, there was no police officer who considered him to be a threat. And he had readily agreed to play second fiddle to the CBI officers.

DARIUS WATCHED THE TELEVISION DRAMA FROM INSIDE HIS hotel room in Bhusaval. He had ordered poha and masala chai to the room, and lit a joint when he saw his mad momma on the screen. He laughed loudly as she spoke, spilling the poha on the bed.

"Come home please, your mother needs you."

The laughter continued. "Mom, you've given a rat's arse for me for all these years, and now you need me? Need me? Hiyuk, hiyuk."

And Darius didn't miss the little chemistry between the elderly cop and his darling mother. Clearly it was this dude who was on his trail, "and it must have been the same fucker who got my mother to this reality show." He saw the name rolling on the ticker. Azeem Khan.

"Okay Khan Uncle, you want to play this little game? You want to fuck with Darius Irani? I'm on, chief."

But first, Darius needed to get an urgent makeover. His smiley face was on all the channels. "Savio, you dog, couldn't you shut the fuck up?"

Using the drain pipe, he slipped out of the first floor window, and quietly walked to the road. Darius was wearing a cap and a false moustache he had kept on standby for a time like this. He looked for a chemist, and found one easily. He bought a few rolls of medical dressing and a pack of Band-Aid. He headed back to his room, the same way he had left.

Darius wrapped the dressing across his head and face, and pasted a few Band-Aid strips at random spots. He then got ready to check out of the hotel.

"Sorry boss, can't find my identity card. And I slipped on the bathroom floor and hurt myself very badly. The tiles have cracked at many places, and they need to be changed. Thankfully, I carry a medical kit, else I would have called for an ambulance."

The receptionist cum manager, not keen on solving the customer's medical issues, and worried that he might claim damages, was only too happy to let the man go off as soon as possible. Darius walked to the station; he had to catch a train out of this boring village called Bhusaval. "*Bhosraval*", he had been chuckling to himself. But before that, he needed to make a phone call.

THE CRIME BRANCH'S TELEPHONE OPERATOR WAS BREATHLESS.

"Mr. Khan, this man wants to speak to you, he says he's the serial killer. Should I put him through?"

"Yes, and while I'm talking, ask the guys to trace the call." Khan had been hoping for this moment to arrive ever since he had begun working on the case. He liked talking to murderers; it always thrilled him. And if this was a crank call from a man with lots of time to spare, he'd track down the loser and chop off his tongue.

"Hello, who's speaking?"

"Is that Azeem Khan?"

"Yes."

The heavy voice and the brutal frankness startled the battle-hardened Khan.

"Dude, I am the lady killer. Come and catch me if you have the balls. Don't drag my mother into this, I give a fuck about her anyway."

Khan lit a cigarette. "Darius, you are making a mistake. Surrender to the nearest police station in your location. We will try and do the best we can to save you."

The response was laughter, mocking laughter. "Save? Only Jesus saves, man, and you are a coward. *Gaand mein dum hai toh maidan mein aaja.* I bloody challenge you, old man."

"Take it easy, Darius, what you are doing is not right…"

Khan could not complete the sentence. He was worried the call would be disconnected at any moment, and he needed to say something to this crazed man to prevent him from attacking another woman. But it didn't work.

"Not right? Who the fuck are you to decide that? Are you my pop? Are you my mom's lover? You fuck with me, I fuck with you. Listen dude, I am going to do it again. Move fast, your ass is on fire."

The phone went dead.

"Sir, the call was traced to Bhusaval railway station!" An excited officer arrived to inform Khan, hoping for a pat on the back. But the latter knew the information was useless. Darius would have been long gone by the time the local cops reached the spot.

"Should I call my colleagues at Bhusaval?" It was Kamble this time.

"Screw it. Waste of time."

He was right. Darius had already boarded a train without bothering to check where it was headed. A kindly passenger offered the badly injured man his seat, which Darius graciously accepted. But there was rage in his head. He had hated the police officer's condescending tone. He would have liked it if the old chap had been abusive.

"You don't get preachy with Darius. You do, you pay."

KHAN IMMEDIATELY CALLED A MEETING INSIDE AHLUWALIA'S room. He looked worried.

"Gentlemen, this man is completely wild. He is going to strike again. Where, I don't know. But he will, very soon. I can feel it in my bones. And the real bad news is that he gives a shit about his mother."

On the last point, all of them agreed. And they played the recorded conversation a few times. There was silence in the room.

"Any thoughts, anyone?"

Ahluwalia was more concerned about following protocol. "Khan, I hope you'll share this with the CBI?"

"Yes, a copy of the recording is already on its way to them. In fact, they called to say they will conduct their own investigation in Bhusaval."

Sushant Singh shrugged his shoulders. "He could end up in any city or town. The problem is, we can't predict anything. There is no pattern to his work."

Kamble, trying to go one up, walked to the whiteboard and drew a chart.

Delhi

Goa

Bangalore

Pune

They stared at the board, but could see no pattern. Ahluwalia, a bit irritated, said they had been through this rubbish before, and it was clear they were dealing with a killer who operated randomly. "You guys have been watching too many Hollywood films. This pattern nonsense happens only in that world."

Khan replied. "Perhaps. But we do know it's a new city each time. He's not repeating a city, and he's favouring large cities."

"Which is why Chennai and Kolkata have already been alerted," Kamble chipped in.

Singh raised his hand. "What about Mumbai?"

Khan was suddenly struck by a thought that had eluded him all along, only because he had been busy looking at the micro picture. "Yes, what about Mumbai? Guys, isn't it odd that Darius hasn't killed in the city he belongs to? The city he knows best?"

Ahluwalia reasoned that it could be because of the fear of being recognised. "Perhaps he thinks he has a better chance of success in alien places."

"I don't think so, Jasjit. Can't you make out from the way the guy was barking on the phone that he gives a damn about such things? Let's try and get into this bastard's mind, that's the only way we can possibly predict anything."

After a few minutes of silence, Khan looked at Singh. "You're right. I think he will hit Mumbai next."

Ahluwalia looked puzzled. "How can you be so sure?"

"Notice what he said. *Gaand mein dum hai toh maidan mein aaja.* He's looking for the thrill of a challenge. He is also angry, perhaps because we've managed to identify him."

"And so?"

"So the real thrill for a man like him would be to fuck with us in our own backyard. I think he's looking to be a daredevil, and there's no daredevilry in killing a poor girl in Guwahati. Kamble, send out teams to scour the airport and all the railway stations, bus stops and entry points."

THE BRAND NEW REFRIGERATOR BROUGHT SOME DESPERATELY needed joy to the Irani household, even though Jeroo was depressed and worried about her missing son. New appliances have that effect on people, especially those who have never received a gift in their entire lives.

She reached into the LG Double Door Frost Free and drank chilled water straight from the bottle. This provided instant relief. Her ancient Godrej fridge would manage to deliver marginally cold water eighteen hours after loading. Jeroo sat down on the sofa and began thinking about why things had gone so horribly wrong. Perhaps she should have consulted a psychiatrist while Darius was still young and manageable. But how was she to know her son would grow up to be a mind-fucked man? He used to be a genius at school.

And yet, there had been early signs, signs she had ignored. Like the day when her 12-year-old son landed a blow on her face only because she had fooled around with his books. And had barked those filthy words, words that she didn't know Darius had even heard of, leave alone master. Perhaps she should have sought help right then. "But where was the money to pay these blood-sucking doctors?" she consoled herself.

If only Ronnie hadn't been such a loser, if only he had been a good dad, if only he had lived, things would surely have been different. She remembered that violent night. The punch-up between the husband and wife in full view of their startled five-year-old. All that blood-letting. Surely that night would have left deep scars on a growing mind. "Perhaps it's not Darius's fault, the way he's turned out."

Tears dripped down her crease-lined cheeks. Yes, the parents had fucked up. And now there was a monster on the loose. Jeroo was suddenly struck with an emotion she didn't know she possessed. Guilt. She reached out for another helping of the chilled water. LG: Life's Good.

KHAN WAS ALONE IN THE ROOM. HE GLANCED ONCE AGAIN AT the soft board scribbles. And began to think, hard.

Darius will come to Mumbai. Where will he stay? A seedy hotel? A friend's place? No, the former was more likely. He would have known the police had busted the hash gang; the Bangalore wedding pictures were all over the media. And he'd guess his other contacts would also be under surveillance. Also, Darius would surely be decked up in a brand new disguise. There had been no tip-off from Bhusaval, so clearly, no one had noticed the chap.

As Khan read and re-read his earlier notes, desperately searching for some sort of clue, he remembered Jahanbux Irani, who was still in custody.

"Poor old man, I must let him go." He then added one more thought on the soft board.

Are you my pop? Are you my mom's lover?
Indicative of a child who's grown up in a troubled home. Jeroo may be concealing dark secrets.
You fuck with me, I fuck with you.
Revengeful.

Revengeful. The word got stuck in Khan's head, and he pondered for a while. "What if? And if so, I can't take a chance." He called Kamble on his cell phone.

"That girl, Imogen Parsons's friend, what was her name?"

"Geeta Kulkarni."

"Text me her number and post one constable outside her house and one outside her office."

There was a pause, just for a second. Kamble wasn't sure why that idiotic girl needed protection. She didn't know anything about anything, and she was a damned liar to boot. He hadn't forgotten the woman had made him look like a fool in front of his peers. Kamble had a choice Marathi cuss word ready for Geeta, but swallowed it. "Yessir."

JAHANBUX IRANI WASN'T EXACTLY IN GOOD SPIRITS, AND despite being aware he was talking to a senior officer of the crime branch, he gave Khan a mouthful.

"What the hell am I still doing here? What do you buggers want from me? I did not produce Darius, that useless woman did. Go lock her up! I loaned my criminal nephew some money, and that was my only mistake, dammit."

Khan did not react. He knew a slanging match with the old gentleman would be a waste of time and energy.

"Mr. Irani, you are free to go, sorry for the trouble. A cab is being called to drop you to your home in Pune."

"Ah, about time! Thank you very much for small mercies. And who will compensate me for all the thievery my assistant must have done in my store? She has been eyeing my cashbox for a long time." Khan ignored the cribbing. He had more pressing issues on his mind.

"Before you go, one final request. Describe Jeroo Irani in one sentence."

"She's a bloody witch. What Darius has become today is only because of her."

"How did your brother die?"

"He had a liver problem because of all the drinking he did to handle all the crap his wife would fart all day. After his death, I broke all ties with that family, but that rascal Darius would occasionally spring up for cash."

"Do you think Darius suffers from schizophrenia?"

"I don't know, maybe he does. Who would not with a crazy mother like that?"

"Okay, Mr. Irani, you can leave. Thanks for all your help, and if you hear from Darius, you know what to do."

"Yes, that bugger Kamble told me. By the way, that fellow stinks so much; ask him to bathe every day."

Jahanbux Irani stood up and walked to the door. He suddenly turned around.

"Soon after my brother died, there were rumours doing the rounds in Colaba that Jeroo had killed Ronnie. Ask the witch about that."

AS REPORTS OF MORE MURDERS HAD POURED IN, GEETA'S mental health nose-dived. She was always looking over her shoulder, and now the killer's face had begun to haunt her. She would often wonder what the beautiful Imogen saw in this crazy man. The stress had begun to take a toll on the art director's work and her boss had expressed disappointment on several occasions.

And that meant Geeta had one more worry on hand – that of losing her job. She did not have the enthusiasm or the energy to look for a job at another advertising agency. And Geeta knew her life would be over in sleepy Nagpur. Her folks would force her to marry a conservative dude, and she'd spend the rest of her life cooking *puran polis* for the loser and his down-market family. That life she certainly did not want. Death was preferable.

And soon, the inevitable happened. Her boss, the creative group head, asked her out to dinner. Geeta knew this was a golden handshake invitation. When the usually reticent Piyush Roy asked you out, your goose was cooked. Geeta had to do something fast and something desperate to prevent it; this job was the only thing going for her.

They hired a cab to get to Copper Chimney restaurant, and on the way, in the midst of cribbing about an unreasonable client, Geeta took her chance. There was nothing to lose anyway, as she was sure she would be jobless in the next hour or so. She slid her hand over Piyush's crotch. At first the boss was taken aback, but then decided to sit back and enjoy the free ride. Geeta's version of a golden handshake killed the unpleasant development scheduled for the evening.

Her job was safe, but she had to sleep with Piyush now and then. He was no longer the classy man he projected himself to be in the office. He was just another lusty fucker who got lucky. The guy was a lousy lover, but Geeta didn't really mind that. It was Darius Irani's face that was on her mind all the time. And the sudden call from Khan heightened the anxiety.

"Ms. Kulkarni, Azeem Khan speaking. Did Darius try to reach you again?"

"What? No sir. Why do you ask?"

"Well, let me know immediately if he calls you. Also, don't be alarmed, I have posted security for you, just to be safe."

Geeta was in a panic. "But why, is my life in danger? What the hell did I do?"

"Relax miss, you did nothing. It's just a precaution."

"But why would he be interested in me? I did no wrong!" She was on the edge now, worried that the police had discussed her with the serial killer.

Khan made the effort to sound as calm as possible, though he was anxious. "I know that, Geeta. We are just being extra cautious, that's all."

The frightened art director felt she was going to have a nervous breakdown, and she desperately wanted someone by her side. She texted Piyush, who was in his cabin, facing her glass cubicle.

"Cn I sty @ yr pad tonite? Wanna hv fun? :)"

":) :) Okie. C u across d road at 8. Same spot."

IT WAS EARLY IN THE MORNING. A HEAVILY BANDAGED DARIUS stood at the entrance to the Pune-Mumbai Expressway, sipping from a Pepsi can. He had switched trains, boarded the Gorakhpur Pune Express, and had then decided to hitch a ride. He was keeping a hawk's eye on the drivers racing by. Darius had a particular characteristic in mind.

About a hundred vehicles had gone by, with no one bothering to offer a ride to a badly injured man.

"Bastards," Darius had yelled after them. He finally found his target. A middle-aged man in a Maruti Swift driving by himself. Darius started gesticulating frantically, and rushed dangerously close to the vehicle.

"Help, help, please help!"

The stunned driver braked hard and skidded to a halt. Thankfully there was no vehicle trailing him. Before he could react, the hitchhiker had swung the front door open, and plonked himself on the passenger seat.

"Sir, please help me, I need to reach a hospital in Mumbai. I had a very bad accident. The small-time doctor out here has provided temporary treatment. Lord Hanuman will bless you." Darius had spotted the hanger on the rear view mirror.

The portly man hesitated. He was hung over, having consumed many drinks the previous night, but that didn't make him forget the recent incidents of mugging on the Expressway.

"But those involved villagers; this guy looks like an educated, decent, city-bred chap, and is in a bad shape anyway," he quickly considered. The man agreed to drive the injured stranger to Mumbai, and started the car.

"What happened to you?"

"Had a bad accident with a truck. My car is totally damaged, but I am alive."

"Mumbai is far away. Perhaps I should drop you off at Lonavala. There are a couple of hospitals there, which aren't too bad."

"Thanks buddy, but my dad has already booked a room at Breach Candy. I trust that hospital."

The hospital's name had the necessary effect, and the driver began to relax. "Music? Just to soothe you a little?"

"No, I'm okay, really. Thanks. Think I'll doze off, if you don't mind."

Darius planned to flash his knife and separate the man from his booty as soon as they reached Mumbai. The bloke looked like a loaded businessman, so at the very least, a few thousand rupees would be on offer. But he changed his mind, as he didn't want to create news for the wrong reasons. There were bigger fish to fry.

The ride was uneventful. The man had stopped to use the toilet at a food court. All that booze needed draining. Darius sat in the car, and noticed that the chap had left the key in the ignition. He was tempted to zip off, and had to fight the feeling down. He lit a cigarette. The man saw him smoking as he returned, still adjusting his zipper, a typical Indian male habit. Darius didn't give him a chance to express surprise.

"Sorry boss, the stress is killing me. Better to die of cancer after some years than to pop it right now outside a highway food court." He flashed the trademark Darius Irani smile. The smile that had melted many a heart.

A constable stared into the car at the Mumbai police check post. The spot was bustling with security personnel, and every vehicle was being scanned. He saw a fat man transporting an injured passenger.

"What's your name?"

"Saurabh Shah."

"And who's this?"

"Sir, he was badly injured in a highway accident, and I'm taking him to Breach Candy hospital."

The cop glanced at the passenger, and saw a heavily bandaged man curled up in pain, shivering, his eyes shut. The car behind honked, and the furious constable turned to glare at the driver who had dared to show impatience at the check post.

"Ok, go." And he rushed to slap the honk-loving driver.

Outside the Breach Candy hospital, after the good-byes were done, Darius hailed a cab. To get to a small shop located at Lamington Road. They stocked the stuff that he needed urgently.

PIYUSH ROY LIVED IN AN OLD BUILDING IN BANDRA. HE WAS A single man, and therefore the rented apartment was always a mess.

Geeta had commented on this on a previous visit and so, Piyush had decided to tidy up a little bit, at least the bed. He didn't like to see her frown during foreplay.

They drove to his apartment, parked the car and climbed to the second floor. The building was equipped with a rickety elevator, but the very private Piyush hated running into neighbours, even when he was alone. Tonight, he would definitely not like that.

After sipping a glass of red wine, the couple moved to the bedroom.

"Ah, the room looks neat tonight, Piyush. Expecting someone?" She giggled as it was her way of beating stress. And Piyush liked it when she giggled like that. He had a fetish for little girls, and when Geeta behaved like one, it turned him on. He grabbed her and they jumped onto the bed. They made love, and then Geeta lit a cigarette.

"Marry me, Piyush."

He laughed loudly, and she giggled again. Geeta had picked up the effect it was having on her boss. He jumped on her and went inside again, even as the lady smoked. She didn't really mind it. Sex romps with Piyush did two things. One, help Geeta retain her job. Two, keep her mind off Imogen's murderer.

A few minutes later, Geeta's silent phone began to vibrate; it was her mother. As usual, she wanted to know where her daughter was. Mrs. Kulkarni of Nagpur had always worried that a rogue advertising man would lead her simple, innocent daughter astray. She would call every single day to reassure herself.

"Where are you, *beta*?"

Geeta smiled. She fondled the hair on Piyush's chest. Another turn-on button for the ad man. "Getting my eyebrows trimmed, *aai*." She pulled at the chest hair, and her companion suppressed a moan.

"Okay, but go home after that, it's already dark. Mumbai is not a safe city anymore. It's full of evil men."

Geeta let her hand wander down Piyush's body. "Don't worry, *aai*. I know exactly how to handle evil Mumbai men." She disconnected the call, and burst out laughing. Imogen was all forgotten in that moment. So was sleepy Nagpur.

JUST THEN A BEARDED MAN WEARING DARK GLASSES ARRIVED at the building gate. He was holding a shopping bag. The sole watchman disinterestedly enquired who the visitor wanted to meet. Glares at night didn't freak Shivpal Singh, a migrant from Etawah. He had been working in Bandra for three years, and had seen many such 'cartoons' before. That's how he described Mumbai lads in his letters to his wife, who he had left behind to raise three kids by herself.

The answer was businesslike. "Piyush Roy."

"*Theek hai. Entry maaro.*" The UP *bhaiyya* had picked up the local lingo. The visitor signed and went up. Singh didn't bother to check what was entered in the dusty register; they didn't pay him to do that. Rather, he was chuckling to himself, having guessed that Piyush *saab's* party just got pooped. And the watchman was right.

The doorbell rang and Piyush immediately belted out swear words. "What the fuck? Who the fuck? Why do people like to disturb others? No fucking peace in this city, I tell you."

Geeta smiled. "Must be the wife you've kept hidden from me."

Piyush quickly put on his trousers, without bothering with his underwear. He had just been turned on again and the bulge was visible, but he didn't care. All he wanted was to give a piece of his mind to the damned intruder. The creative director was usually a peace-loving man, but this nuisance certainly wasn't going to be tolerated.

He didn't even get a chance to look at the uninvited bell ringer. The attack was lightning fast, and death was almost instantaneous. The knife pierced the side of his neck, and the lifeless, shirtless body of Piyush Roy dropped to the floor with a soft thud, the pelvic bulge still to completely subside. The Persian carpet had muffled the sound. Darius didn't miss the die-hard erection. He stamped on it as if it was a slithering vermin.

Geeta didn't hear a thing, and that surprised her. She was expecting a shout fest. She was lying on the bed, naked, smoking a cigarette when the stranger softly walked in. He was grinning widely.

"Hi honey bunny, sorry to disturb."

THE BODIES WERE DISCOVERED TWO DAYS LATER, AFTER A neighbour complained of a foul smell emanating from the apartment. Uncollected newspapers were lying outside the door, and when that happens, it usually spells disaster in Mumbai. The society manager decided to call the cops.

Once again, the media went mad. They had new bones to chew on. The TV anchors were screaming their guts out.

"The police is a disaster, and so is the CBI, the nation's last hope in crime investigation!"

"The killer has become bold enough to slaughter two people at one go!"

"The nation has gone to the dogs!"

The Home Minister feigned chest pains, and demanded that the CBI chief face the music. Iyengar was on all the channels the next day, sportingly taking abuses from the news anchors, while quietly cursing the Minister. The portly anchor, as usual, was having the most fun.

"How can you let this happen, Mr. Iyengar, the nation demands an answer! Are your officers sleeping? How many more deaths will it take for you to wake up? Will you resign tonight?"

This was followed by heated debates with the usual television suspects.

Egged on by the raging media, activists and assorted do-gooders were back on the streets in all the metro towns, armed with placards and candles. Anti-social elements decided to join the party. A few cars were torched, and there were violent protests below Jeroo Irani's building. The Prime Minister decided to switch to a comedy show on television. Effective de-stressors they were. He watched these when he found himself in a sticky situation, which was often these days.

Zeenat called her husband and demanded that he pack up and leave. "Right Now!" SMSes wouldn't do anymore, and she had had enough of this nonsense.

"Let the bloody CBI deal with this shit!" she screeched.

Kamble was at the crime scene, quietly watching twenty CBI officers and many more forensics experts investigate the twin murders. He concealed a grin when he saw two officers rain punches on the watchman Shivpal Singh. He was amused not just because he knew this was a pointless exercise carried on out of frustration, but he also loved it when migrants from the north of India got assaulted. He hated these guys, and wanted them out of 'his' city.

Of course, Shivpal Singh hadn't bothered to check the register entry; of course, he hadn't asked for the visitor's name; of course, he hadn't checked the purpose of the man's visit; of course, he hadn't insisted the cartoon remove his glares. And of course, he had overlooked the visitor's resemblance to the serial killer. He wasn't paid for or briefed on all these things, the watchman meekly protested.

And tonight he was going to sleep on the terrace with a bloodied nose and severe aches in his legs. And wonder whether farming in Etawah wasn't such a bad idea after all.

Worse, it had taken forty-eight hours to discover the corpses. Darius Irani could be anywhere by now. Stuffing himself with mutton biryani at Lucky Restaurant located next door, or enjoying a hash yatra in Ibiza. The CBI officers knew they were pretty much screwed. All the *nakabandis* that had been ordered weren't going to help. Neither would angry calls from their bosses in Delhi.

KHAN WAS READING THE NEWSPAPERS THE NEXT MORNING IN his hotel room. The excited room service boy, elated to have such an esteemed guest in the hotel, had been annoying him with questions on the killer. It was getting on Khan's nerves, but he always managed a smile. In his younger days, he might have swatted the pest.

It was the same story. Geeta Kulkarni's murder carried a trademark: Deed Done By Darius Rohington Irani. And this time he had used a television remote control sourced from Piyush Roy's living room. Like Kamble, Khan understood the futility of leg work. Darius was long gone, and the investigation process would be a complete waste of time. He had to do the only thing he had been hired to do: Think of a way to either ensnare the culprit or preempt his next move. The only real hope was that someone would recognise this man and raise an alarm, but the genius Darius had managed to fool everyone with simple disguises. There was of course the other option, one that would sort out Khan's messed-up life: Concede defeat, chuck it all up, and go home to sweet Coonoor.

Khan thought of Shraddha, and suddenly felt like a hug.

"Perhaps I should call her tonight."

He fixed a large whisky, unmindful of the time the wall clock reported. 8.15 a.m. Khan called for the room service boy, and gave him a few hundred bucks.

"Get as many Gold Flake Kings as you can."

He lit a cigarette from his nearly finished pack, and began to think. Khan needed to think laterally,

"Like that creative director would do," he said to himself.

The creative director who died a pointless death only because he chose to bonk the wrong chick. Darius would describe him as 'necessary collateral damage, but fun to do anyway'.

After a couple of hours, he had an idea. Khan picked up the cell phone which he had placed on silent mode. He noticed there were five missed calls from Zeenat and two from Jasjit Ahluwalia. He ignored them and called Kamble.

"Bring Sushant and come to my hotel room as soon as possible. Which is like right now."

He disconnected without waiting for a response, and continued drinking.

FULLY NAKED, GEETA LIT ANOTHER CIGARETTE WHILE SHE waited for her partner to return. She felt hungry after all the hard work done for the boss, and there was more work to be done for the horny man. Geeta was contemplating dinner options when her thoughts were disturbed by a polite voice.

She saw a tall, handsome, curly-haired man, wearing a blue checked shirt and black jeans, cheerfully smiling down at her. Shell-shocked, Geeta took a few seconds to recover. Then she mechanically looked for a bedsheet to cover herself with and finding none, grabbed a couple of pillows.

"Who are you? How did you get in here? Get out of the room!" She screamed for her boss.

The intruder burst out laughing. "No use love, he just exited from the world with his hard-on intact. Now it's just me and you, and we need to bond."

And then it struck her. It was the same rugged, threatening voice she had heard on the phone. Imogen's fatal mistake had arrived at Geeta's doorstep. She shrivelled up in the bed, dazed, confused, scared, unsure of what her next action should be. Jumping off from the bed, fully unclothed, in front of a murderous man, was not a sensible option. But she couldn't just lie there, waiting for something to happen.

Darius, as if reading her mind, stood silently, smiling, staring down at her. As one would at a caged animal in a zoo, patiently waiting, wondering what the beast might do. She tried to reach for her cell phone, but it proved futile. Darius was on top of her in a flash. Before Geeta could register the new development, three things happened almost in one motion. With one hand he crushed the phone, as one would an empty cigarette pack, and threw it away. With the other, he bummed a cigarette from her pack, and lit it. And he robbed the woman of the two things that were helping cover her dignity: the pillows. Darius was now sitting on her stomach, smoking and sniggering at her little breasts.

"Right, Geeta fucking Kulkarni, it's confession time. Did you reveal my identity to the police?"

Stunned by the sudden turn of events, her brain, still half-processing dinner options, wasn't functioning fully. Geeta found herself shivering and stammering.

"No, no, I did not. I didn't even know your name; they found that out from somewhere else."

Darius clamped his hand on her mouth. With the other, he pressed the lit cigarette on her left breast, at the centre of the nipple. In response he heard muffled sounds of great pain. Darius was smiling. These sounds brought peace to his mind.

"I am going to remove my hand. Scream, and I shall poke the cigarette into your left eye. Are we clear?" She managed a nod.

"Geetakins, all I want is the truth, and nothing but the truth, so help me babe. And then I shall let you go, I promise. Even if you didn't know my name, you did speak to the cops about our conversation, despite my clear warning. Naughty girl."

The art director managed a pained whisper.

"Yes, that was a big mistake, please forgive me, please. They tricked me into it. I have done you no wrong."

"Was it Azeem Khan?"

She nodded, hoping, desperately hoping this feedback would get the mad man off her case, and more importantly, off her body, which he was still using as a stool.

Instead, Geeta heard hysterical laughter. "Well, darling, you did make a big mistake. The other chicks hadn't wronged me in any way and they still had to go. You deserve a bonus from Santa Darius."

This time he stubbed the cigarette on her other nipple. But he saved Geeta the new pain as a heavy object cracked her skull.

While leaving, Darius struck gold. Rummaging through Piyush's cupboard, he found three lakh rupees in cash and a few hundred US dollars.

"The dude mustn't have paid taxes on this dosh. Imagine cheating the country and bonking its virgins for free. Such trash needs to die." He spat on the dead man's face as he walked out the door.

KHAN EXPLAINED THE PLAN. HE HAD TO WIN THE MAD JEROO over. The two had already developed a little relationship, but it wasn't enough. He needed to know everything about Darius. Everything. And that would only happen if Jeroo developed a great deal of trust in Khan.

The glass of Scotch in Khan's hand early in the morning had surprised the two officers. Singh was beginning to worry about the old man.

"That's fine sir, but how will it help us catch the killer? He can't even contact his mother, neither of them use phones. Or are you suspecting he might visit her?"

Kamble completed the thought. "And if he does, we have a battery of cops all over Colaba. And there are CBI men, too. He'll walk right into the trap."

Both men smiled at each other. As subordinates do when they know the boss has lost it completely.

"Kamble, don't grin like a fool. Your idiotic constables did fuck-all to save Geeta's life, remember? The least they should have done was to alert you after she went MIA. Hope you've suspended the fuckers. Anyway, what's done is done, let's get to the point. I have a feeling Darius will call me again. Geeta was killed because she spoke to us. This was not fun killing, which this insane man usually does. This was revenge killing."

"And so?"

"And so if he calls me, and comes to know I'm aware of his dirty little secrets, two things can happen. He'll either screw up, or he'll put his plans of murdering people on hold. That will give us some breathing space."

Kamble didn't appear convinced, and wasn't pleased with the rebuke, aware that Singh would have enjoyed the side show. He asked what was expected of them in order to win the old hag's affection.

"It's simple. We do exactly what actors do in the movies to win their object of interest's affection. Get together some *taporis* from Colaba, the really loutish ones. Send them to her door, ask them to smash it open, instruct one to put a knife to the woman's neck, and I will appear in the nick of time."

The crime branch officers were convinced it was the booze talking. Kamble decided to get the juvenile plan done with anyway.

AND IT HAD THE RIGHT EFFECT. ALL JEROO HAD RECEIVED FROM human beings in all these years was derision. From neighbours, shopkeepers, cobblers, bus conductors, even beggars. This was an entirely new feeling. Despite her agony over Darius's freelance activities, Khan's 'rescue act' brought joy to her heart. She wanted to hug him tight, but knew she smelled bad and avoided it. Jeroo Irani didn't wish to risk screwing up the one good thing that had happened in her life.

She offered Khan a cup of tea, which was accepted.

"Is black tea fine?"

Khan was more than happy. He didn't need milk after all that Scotch in his system; he also figured there might be no milk supply in the Irani household.

"Thank you once again sir, you are a good man."

"You're most welcome. I had actually come to ask you a few more questions, hope you don't mind."

"Yes, please ask. Anything that can help find my son. Only promise me once again that your men won't kill him."

"Yes, I promise. Ma'am, be totally honest as the correct information will help us minimise the punishment for your son. Did Darius have a troubled childhood? Was his father good to him?"

Jeroo perked up, as if she had been waiting a long time for someone to ask this question.

"No, I'm sorry to say that Ronnie was not a good father. He would often hit Darius over small matters like spending too much time in the bathroom or breaking a vessel… things like that. I would try to stop him, but Ronnie was a hot-tempered man, and he was always drunk."

"Was he violent with you as well?"

"Yes, all the time. I suffered fractures in my arms and legs on numerous occasions. And my private parts got permanently damaged." Khan waited for a few seconds before continuing with the conversation.

"Sorry to hear about that. And how would young Darius react when he saw him assaulting you?"

"Very badly. He would cry, he would hide under the bed, and…", she tapered off.

"And?"

"He would urinate in his pyjamas. Once he wet the bed, and Ronnie went completely mad. He beat the poor boy black and blue, and our neighbours had to call the police. After that incident, Darius was hardly seen at home. He would sit in the school compound for hours after classes were over, or he would roam around on the streets. That's how he fell into bad company."

"Mrs. Irani, how exactly did your husband die? Sorry to ask this question, but I need to know. And trust me, the right answer will help Darius's case in the court of law. Was he responsible for his father's death?"

"No sir, absolutely not! Darius was too young to do anything. My husband was an alcoholic, and he died of liver cirrhosis. I have his death certificate kept somewhere. Do you want to see it? Should I search for it?"

"No, there's no need for that, I'm sure you are speaking the truth. One last question: Didn't you seek medical help for your son? Children raised in a violent family often need help from professionals."

"Mr. Khan, my husband left me no money. It's a miracle we have managed to survive. Had it not been for your kind heart, I would never have seen a new fridge in my house. How could I afford fees for these expensive doctors, they are all blood suckers! But recently, with a relative's help, I organised a free consultation with a psychiatrist."

"And?"

"Nothing came of it, and the poor doctor died of a heart attack shortly afterward."

Khan nodded, having sensed rightly that Darius had something to do with it. He thanked Jeroo for the tea and left satisfied. He was convinced this had been a useful meeting.

DARIUS IRANI WAS BACK IN DELHI, AND THIS TIME IN A SIKH avatar. No one paid any attention to a strapping sardarji walking around Connaught Circus. He bought a few newspapers and magazines, and walked into Nirula's for lunch, to quietly gloat over all the attention being showered upon him. He laughed out loudly on the 'insightful' comments offered by the nation's chatterati, and received inquisitive glances from guests seated at other tables.

As he was loaded with cash, Darius wanted to check into a luxury hotel and chill out for a few days. But that would need proof of identity, which meant some work had to be done before he could get to dive into the satin bedsheets and place an order for single malt on the rocks.

"I deserve a bit of indulgence. I am India's Most Wanted Man, after all."

Darius walked around the various blocks of the Circus, staring at the pretty girls he saw along the way. "Not now Darius, there's work to be done, behave yourself."

And soon he found what he was looking for. In the parking lot, he saw a middle-aged Sikh gentleman open the door of his Skoda Octavia. He appeared ready to drive away. Darius read the car's Haryana registration number, and decided to take a chance.

"Sirji, if you don't mind, could you please guide me? I'm lost."

The man stared at Darius, surprised to meet a fellow Sikh who spoke in a strange accent. Darius sorted out that issue pretty quickly.

"I'm an NRI based in Canada. This is my first visit to India in thirty years. Therefore, please pardon me, I don't speak Punjabi."

Real estate agent Kuljeet Singh warmed up immediately. "Ah, that's fine, no problem. What can I do for you? Always happy to help brothers from foreign countries."

"I have to meet an aunt in Gurgaon, and I was wondering what's the best way to get there. Does the metro go to Gurgaon, or will I have to hire a cab?"

Darius had found his mark. The man was now smiling cheerfully, and he placed his hand on the stranger's shoulder.

"Oye, you have come to the right man, *paaji*. I am from Gurgaon, and I'm going there right now. If you want, you can come with me."

"That would be very nice, sirji, as long as it's no trouble for you. My mother had said to me if I needed any help in Delhi, I must approach a Sikh brother. She was so right."

"No trouble at all, my friend. In fact, time will pass quickly as we chat along the way, especially about beautiful Canadian ladies. I like making new friends. Hi, I'm Kuljeet." He extended one hand, which was received warmly by the lost NRI.

"Hi, I'm Rajinder Singh Bindra. So nice to meet you."

JEROO BOUGHT A BOTTLE OF THE CHEAPEST RED WINE FROM the booze shop down the street. She tried to avoid eye contact with the shop attendant, but he recognised her immediately. Not wanting to engage with this crazy mother of a crazy son, he ignored the thirsty men thronging his shop and served her first.

Unknown to the woman, two CBI sleuths had followed her to the shop and then back to her house. Below the building, a couple of lads made snide remarks, but Jeroo didn't notice. They were quietly dealt with by the men following her. The cops wondered if her famous son was planning to join her for a drink, and hid behind a wall to keep an eye out.

It had been many years since Jeroo treated herself to wine. Even though she preferred it at room temperature, she dunked many ice cubes in her glass. What was the point of the new LG if it wasn't put to use? After a couple of refills, she mulled over her conversation with Khan.

"Did he believe me? I think he did. I hope he did. Too much happening already; my son is in big trouble, and I cannot risk skeletons tumbling out."

As she continued to sip her ice-cold wine, Jeroo's mind raced back to those horrid days. Violence in the house. Little Darius wetting his shorts. The useless Ronnie, the bloody loser.

"In a way I'm happy he went early, it put an end to the beatings. But should I have told that policeman everything? Would that have helped my son's case?"

Jeroo finished the bottle of wine and limped to the bed. She did not feel like eating, and wanted to pass out pissed drunk. That night she felt haunted.

JUST AT THAT MOMENT, HER SON CHECKED INTO THE BRISTOL Hotel, Gurgaon, courtesy Piyush Roy. And a little later, he was rocking in the soft bed while munching on the kebab platter he had ordered with the 16-year-old Lagavulin. And the good time he was having got better when he switched on the television set. All the news channels were hotly discussing Darius Irani. He was in splits when a socialite offered to conduct a personality analysis of the killer.

The hour-long drive with Kuljeet Singh had been a delight. He was a funny man, full of hilarious anecdotes about life in New Delhi. He revealed new tricks his gang had picked up after the clampdown on sexual perverts, and expounded on the art of molesting girls on the streets without being caught. Singh called it the 'hit and run strategy'. Darius liked him a lot, and if this had been Colaba, he most certainly would have invited this guy over to his house for an all-night booze binge. Mom, of course, would have thrown a fit, but that was part of the fun.

But today, he had work to do with Kuljeet Singh. Once Darius came to know the driver was a real estate agent, he expressed interest in buying an apartment in a Gurgaon high-rise. It had the desired effect. Kuljeet's smile had gotten wider, the jokes louder, and he insisted brother Rajinder drop by the office for *lassi* before progressing to his aunt's pad. Along the way, Darius asked for the car to be stopped at a medical store, as he needed to purchase headache pills. In order to please a potential customer, the agent offered to do the honours.

And this gave Darius the opportunity he was waiting for. To fish out Kuljeet Singh's driving licence, which he was hoping would be in the glove box. That would save him the bother of picking the man's pocket. It was there. He checked the date of expiry. It was valid for another three years.

"Cool. The next time this chap looks for his licence will be when he's caught for jumping a signal." And when it was time to say good-bye, Darius felt a tinge of sadness for he really did want to spend more time with this funny man.

"Perhaps another time on an easy day. I need to chill out for a few days, and do nothing."

"Thanks Piyush! Cheers!"

KHAN WAS DRINKING IN THE HOTEL ROOM, YET AGAIN. HE thought of checking on Shraddha, but realised it was late in the day. Her jealous husband would be hovering around.

"Should I polish off that useless man?"

Khan found the idea tempting. That way he could have Shraddha to himself, and they could catch up whenever he visited Mumbai.

There was a knock on the door. Khan was surprised as he had called for nothing. He hoped it wasn't another autograph-hunting bell boy; he had had enough of that nonsense. And considering what a failure Khan had been on the assignment so far, he didn't deserve the fan following.

"Surprise!"

Before Khan had a chance to fully register what was happening, Zeenat was already holding him. There was a lit cigarette in his hand, but there was no point in trying to conceal it. His wife would easily win the championship trophy if there was an international contest held to find 'The World's Best Smeller of Foul Odours'. Zeenat was crestfallen.

"What the hell, Khan, what are you doing to yourself? Liquor, cigarettes, what else have you been doing?"

"I've been doing Shraddha" ran in his mind on repeat. Khan knew he was screwed, so he quickly came up with an excuse that usually works with worried wives.

"Zeenat, nice of you to come by, and sorry about all this. I'm really stressed out, as we haven't been able to nab the bastard. I feel like a complete loser."

It worked. She sat down next to him on the sofa and held his hand. "But are you going to be able to catch him if you're drunk? Will messing up your health get you lucky? This is so ridiculous."

As Khan watched helplessly, she collected the cigarette packs and trashed them in the bin. She then gathered the whisky bottles and emptied them in the toilet basin. He was unhappy with this nasty surprise. "Why couldn't Shraddha have given me this surprise?" The thought made him reach for his cell phone, and he switched it to silent mode, just in case.

"Listen, you shouldn't have come here. It's not safe, and I'm terribly tied up."

"Yes, I can smell that. Tied up with all the crap I thought you had left behind."

Later at night, Zeenat tried to get close to him in bed. This is what Khan had been afraid of, but he had to respond or his wife would return to Coonoor, suspicious and unhappy. He made love to her, thinking of Shraddha.

A FEW DAYS WENT BY UNEVENTFULLY AND THIS GAVE KHAN AN opportunity to take Zeenat around the city to their favourite haunts from the days when they were younger. Shalimar restaurant on Mohammed Ali Road. Golden Star at Charni Road. Pani Puri at Chowpatty beach. It had the desired effect. Zeenat took the flight to Bangalore in a good mood, but left behind strict instructions which made her husband smile.

Media pressure had begun to let up a bit, and attention had shifted to news of another deadly attack in the Kashmir valley. A few terrorists had sneaked into the army barracks and killed six officers while they were asleep. Though the news angered Khan, he felt relieved; he needed media attention off Darius Irani.

What he was waiting for, hoping for, was a call. A call from the serial killer. This time Khan had laid out a trap. He had concluded it was not possible to catch the beast in its den; it had to be lured out with a bait. With no sightings reported either by the police from the various Indian cities, or by the CBI teams, this was the only way to reach him. And Khan wanted it very badly; a one-on-one meeting, a man to man confrontation. In his drunken stupor, Khan had imagined slitting Irani's balls before setting them on fire.

One thing Khan had made up his mind on was: Darius Irani had to be quickly eliminated. It was too dangerous to keep a sharp mind like that inside a lock-up. The court proceedings could take months, and even after getting a conviction, the death sentence would take years to execute, given India's lethargic legal and political machinery. Jail break would be a joke for this intelligent man.

And after a week, the call came. Again, to the crime branch office. And Darius, once again, demanded to speak to Khan and no one else.

"How you doing, Azeembhai? Did Zeenat ma'am have a good time in Mumbai?"

Khan's blood froze in his veins, as did that of the two officers listening to the conversation, as well as Jasjit Ahluwalia. But he hesitated only for a moment. Khan was aware this was no time to let emotions take over; he had to play the only card he had, and it had to be played right now. Or never.

"Darius, I know you had a fucked-up childhood, and I know your dad used to beat you black and blue. I even know you used to piss in your knickers. But that's not the fault of the innocent women you've been killing, it was your loser dad's fault."

Ahluwalia's heavy eyebrows darted up sharply; this was not the way he expected Khan to speak, but he decided to go along, assuming this must be a Khan strategy at play. And it seemed to be working, as there was a long pause at the other end, followed by heavy breathing.

"You fucking son of a bitch. Who the fuck told you all this crap? My goddammed mother? You've been meeting her regularly? Fucker."

Khan had pressed the right button, and he decided to push further. "She told me all your dirty secrets, you scumbag. You are a bloody fucked-up loser and a coward. Meet me and I will show you what being a man means. Killing weak women is the only trick up your sleeve, you bastard." The friendly banter was followed by a brief silence.

"Okay fucker, will see you soon. Watch your ass."

The call was traced to Belgaum in Karnataka. The information was duly passed on to the CBI, but the crime branch team knew the chase was pointless. This master of stealth and disguise would be long gone by the time a local constable reached the public call office.

KHAN HAD BEGUN TO SWEAT PROFUSELY AND COLLAPSED INTO the chair. Kamble and Singh rushed to check on him, followed by Ahluwalia.

"Not to worry, I'm fine, just need a glass of water." Impatient Ahluwalia wanted some quick answers.

"Khan, what the hell was that all about? What's your trip, man?" The deputies were desperate to ask the same question, but weren't sure how to phrase it appropriately. Still, the two had enjoyed the hot discussion, and they would have liked so much to participate in it.

"Jasjit, it's simple, really. I want this guy angry, very angry with me, personally."

"And how will that help? He'll go and kill another woman to let off steam." Ahluwalia was agitated.

"On the contrary. I think his focus will shift to me, and if I understand this man correctly, he's already hatching a plan to kill me."

"And you want him to come after you?"

"Yes, that's the only way to catch this bastard."

Ahluwalia nodded reluctantly. He didn't like the way Khan was handling this problem, but he also realised this could be the only option. "We'll have you surrounded by cops. You'll need protection."

"No, no, don't do that. Let's not make it difficult for this guy to reach me. That would be counterproductive." Khan turned to Singh.

"Sushant, take two men of your choice, ask for whatever ammunition you want, and rush to Coonoor. This son of a bitch knows my wife's whereabouts, and I need her to be safe."

Singh was delighted as he had always wanted to visit Ooty. And he was fed up of Mumbai, its 'low-quantity-and-quality' food, the dirty Kamathipura holes where most of the whores, except Mala, acted pricey. Girls at GB Road were more 'adjusting'. Perhaps he'd smuggle his wife to Coonoor. She would be thrilled, and she'd forgive his long absence. Singh's mind was already buzzing with ideas. "Sir, I shall leave right away."

Ahluwalia wasn't entirely convinced. "Khan, you definitely need some protection. I insist on it."

"Okay, I will take Kamble with me wherever I go, but that's all, not another man. I can deal with this coward, trust me."

UNKNOWN TO KHAN, DARIUS HAD BEEN STALKING HIM. HE had discovered the hotel the retired cop had been stationed at, and had spotted Zeenat with him when the two were out having fun in the city. He later followed Zeenat to the Mumbai airport, and figured she lived in another town. And it hadn't been difficult to find out where.

Darius called the crime branch office at night, aware that Khan wouldn't be around. Changing his voice was easy; he had done that on numerous occasions for school dramatics, an activity he had found most enjoyable. Darius asked for Mr. Azeem Khan, and was told Sahib was not in his office. He pretended to be Mrs. Khan's brother from Lucknow.

"Hello, my sister is in Mumbai and I can't reach her. Khan Sahib's phone is also switched off. Can you please guide me on how to reach her? I have an urgent message from our family doctor."

"What's your name?" The call had been directed to a junior, night-duty constable from Kamble's team.

"Salim. I have to contact my sister very urgently."

"She must be travelling, call her after a few hours. Or try Sahib's number tomorrow."

"Oh, but it's a serious matter. I was told she would be in Mumbai for some more days. Where has she gone, any idea, sir?"

"That I can't say. Maybe she's gone home to Coonoor."

"Okay, thank you so much, I will speak to her later. God bless."

Darius chuckled. "And they call these people the Crime Branch. Buffoons."

'Kuljeet Singh' took the next flight out to Bangalore. Coimbatore is closer to Coonoor, but he chose a big city with its big airport to reduce chances of detection. Piyush Roy's money hadn't run out despite a cool three-day holiday at the Bristol. And the estate agent's driving licence was proving to be quite handy. The only thing Darius was unhappy with was the blue turban as it made his head feel itchy. But it had served him well. No one was looking for a Sikh serial killer.

SUSHANT SINGH, ARMED WITH A COLT, STATIONED HIMSELF outside Zeenat's house along with two constables. It was decided that Singh would be at the house during the day, and his assistants would patrol the venue after sunset. Singh hadn't taken this assignment too seriously.

"For one, Darius would not know the Khans have a house at this hill station, and two, Zeenat, at her age, wouldn't interest this murderer of beautiful women."

Meanwhile, in a Delhi suburb, an extremely delighted Mrs. Singh had begun packing heavily for a long stay in Ooty, a place she had heard of only in the Hindi movies. It dawned on her that her husband wasn't as useless as she had always believed him to be. The two could holiday endlessly at this romantic hill station, bills to be paid by the tax payers.

Zeenat insisted the Singhs occupy the guestroom, but the officer politely declined as he preferred to stay in a modest hotel located nearby. The last thing he wanted was for Mrs. Khan to overhear his wife's constant carping.

The next day, a visitor stealthily arrived at the bungalow in the dead of night. He noticed two men stationed outside the house. One was snoozing on a plastic chair placed right outside the gate, his rifle parked between his legs, like an erect penis. The other one was sprawled on the grass on the lawn. Darius wasn't sure if this one was awake, but it was clear the poor fools were on a very low alert level.

Darius grinned. "Dudes, you don't take Uncle Darius so lightly."

The slaughter was instant and painless. Darius tiptoed behind the constable who was asleep on the chair. He slit his throat in one strike, and then slowly dug the knife in, as one would cut a watermelon. The dead man's head rolled onto the ground. The trespasser collected the rifle, and peeped over the boundary wall to check if the beheaded soldier's comrade had heard the sound. He was in the same position as before.

Darius went face down and slowly crawled in the constable's direction. No sign of life. With one hand he clasped the man's mouth, and with the other, he jabbed the knife straight into his heart. The man's body shivered for ten seconds, and then it was all over. Darius collected his rifle, too.

He walked around the bungalow, and spotted no one else. Darius cut the electric cables of the three lampposts standing tall around the lawn. He then walked to the door, and rang the bell.

IT WAS TWO IN THE MORNING WHEN KHAN'S CELL PHONE WENT off. The retired officer, having got sloshed the previous night, was fast asleep. He woke up with a start, and panicked when he found his wife was on the other end. This was going to be bad news for sure. Zeenat would never call him at this hour, never. She was the sort of wife who put her husband's convenience ahead of her own. Even if the husband was a bloody cheater.

"Zeenat, is everything okay?" It was the question one nervously asks dear ones despite strongly suspecting all isn't okay. In response, he heard laughter, the evil laughter he had heard before, the laughter he dreaded.

"Azeembhai, I am your fan number one. Greetings from the lush, lovely, cool Coonoor."

The voice hit like a thunderbolt, and the officer went numb. But it quickly sank into Khan that D-Day had arrived. Years of dealing with hardened criminals had conditioned his mind to regain composure swiftly. Khan knew criminals fed on their victim's fear, and he must not sound frightened.

"Darius, whatever you do, don't harm my wife. She has done you no harm." This time the laughter was hysterical.

"You gotta be kidding, sirji. I don't do old ladies." More laughter.

"She's fine for now, but that can change very quickly. I have an offer to make: Come to your home alone, unarmed, we'll have a nice chat, and then I'll walk away. That's all I want. A man to man discussion. Sounds fair?"

"Yes, that's fair. I'm on my way, just don't do anything silly."

"Cool. By the way, what happened to your colourful vocabulary? I guess India's bravest police officer is shitting bricks."

Laughter, that cruel, hurtful Darius laughter.

"Can I talk to my wife?"

"Wow, so much love at this stage of life! Khan, you are a dude. Don't worry, after our friendly banter is done, I shall leave you guys alone to make out as much as you oldies want. Though I have to say ma'am is still pretty; she can do better than an ugly old duckling like you."

It took a great deal of effort to control his rage: "Okay, stay put, wait for me."

"Once again, you act smart with me, I slit Zeenat's little throat. As simple as that." The phone went dead.

Khan jumped from the bed, and his first action was to call Singh. He heard an irritated yawn that was clumsily muffled.

"Sushant, where are you?"

"Sir, I am in my hotel room. But don't worry, I have posted two very tough men at the house. All is well."

"Now wake up and listen to me very carefully. Stay in your room till you hear from me again. Don't step out. Am I making myself loud and clear?"

"Er, yes sir. Is everything okay?"

"Fuck all that, just stay put in your bloody room."

ZEENAT, RUDELY WOKEN, AND A BIT ALARMED, WALKED TO THE door and enquired who it was. She tried to peer through the adjoining window, but it was pitch dark outside.

"Madam, very sorry to disturb, the power outside has gone, and we don't have a torch. Can we borrow one?" The voice sounded like that of one of the guards patrolling her house. Zeenat didn't think anything beyond that. She opened the door, and in a flash, Darius was upon her.

"Honey, you shout and you are dead. As a police officer's wife, I expect a show of dignity. Will you scream?"

Zeenat's worst nightmare had come true. And yet, she was aware that shouting for help would only get her grief. The intruder was inside the house, holding her by the waist, staring right into her face, and her best option was to cooperate. The possibility that it was the serial killer her husband had been chasing didn't occur to her, not until he had snatched the phone and made the call.

Darius flashed his blood-soaked knife. "First things first. Be a good girl and get me a hard nylon rope."

Still dazed, she slowly walked to the storage room, and the tall, well-built stranger followed her closely. After a little search, the blue rope was found. Darius gave an affectionate peck on her cheek.

"Honey, I may be an evil guy, but I have a big heart. You will be tied to a chair for several hours, and my conscience demands that I let you pee before that. It's the right thing to do, correct?"

Scared and shivering with cold, Zeenat was extremely thankful. Her bladder felt weak, and she really wanted to use the toilet. Darius trailed her to the bathroom located on the ground floor.

"I'm afraid I can't allow you to latch the door, you might try to do something stupid. But don't worry, I won't peep as I don't like the sight of women peeing. If I wanted to see you naked, I would rip your nightgown in a second."

Zeenat didn't respond; she did as she was ordered. She was relieved to be offered a loo break, and her mind had gone blank at the sudden turn of events at this unearthly hour.

KHAN SIPPED COLD WATER AND DARTED OUT OF THE HOTEL, unnoticed. He spotted a cab, and found the driver sleeping on the backseat. He shook the man hard and the cabbie was not amused.

"Nahin jaane ka hai, phoot idhar se."

Khan pulled him up by the collar. "Police. *Jaldi uth nahin toh steering wheel nikaal ke gaand mein ghusa doonga."*

It worked. Within seconds, the cab was racing in the direction of the airport. In a way, Khan was happy he had encountered an uncouth cabbie as it allowed him to let off some of the pent-up steam. But he had to keep a lid on things; he had been tempted to shoot the bastard dead and drive off with his rickety vehicle.

Khan booked a ticket for the first flight to Bangalore, which was at 6 a.m. There was no direct flight to Coimbatore in the early morning hours. And then he grabbed some tea. Khan had to get his mind thinking straight; there was no place for panic in this situation. Using his identity card, he walked out of the airport and smoked three cigarettes in a row. D-Day had arrived. Glory or defeat awaited; there was no third option. But first, Zeenat had to be protected.

From Bangalore airport, he hired a private cab to Coonoor. It was 8 a.m., and it would take close to eight hours to reach his destination. Khan used the time to carefully plan his moves. And the first item on the agenda was to make sure the rest of his colleagues didn't get a whiff of the new development. Darius meant deadly business, and Khan had to deal with this alone. He texted Ahluwalia.

"Off to Coonoor for a few days. Zeenat unwell, but nothing serious. Will be back soon. Rgrds."

SLEEP-DEPRIVED DARIUS HAD CRASHED OUT ON THE SOFA. Zeenat tried to free herself, but it was a futile effort. She thought about the security personnel, remembered the bloody knife, and assumed the worst. Her mind shifted to the fate that awaited her husband, and she began to weep silently.

As the sun shone through the bright Coonoor sky, Darius lazily arose, and cheerfully smiled at Zeenat, who was wide awake. "Ma'am, would you like some coffee? I'm gate-crashing your kitchen, so don't feel shy to ask. It's your own house." Zeenat, still to fully register the late night shock, shook her head.

In the kitchen, after a quick ransack, he found the ingredients to prepare coffee, a few bananas and a pack of digestive cookies. That's all Darius needed for the busy day ahead. He admired the cleanliness and order in the Khan kitchen. "Wish my moronic mother would come here and see how things are done."

He then participated in a one-way discussion with his prisoner. Zeenat tried her best not to look horrified. It had been ingrained in her that a policeman's wife must always appear calm.

"Don't worry, I'm not going to harm you; you look like a nice lady, a mother I never had. That's of course if your husband behaves himself. I guess you must be dying to know why I killed all those bimbettes. The simple answer is this: They happened to be in the wrong place, poor things. Today, one of us will die, either me or your man, and we may never meet again. So let me take the opportunity to tell you this: The world fucked with me, and I fucked back. Good old action and reaction. If I hadn't fucked back, I would have killed myself. But I'm no loser. Even if I die today, I will win. People will remember me forever. And thanks for the bananas, they were much needed. They will help me retain my shit if I get shot."

Later, Darius went about the house on a recce trip. And collected whatever cash he could lay his hands on. He grinned to himself. "Stealing from a cop's house, how cool is that!"

IT WAS ELEVEN IN THE MORNING AND SINGH, HAVING consumed three helpings of idli and chutney, was beginning to feel restless. His wife was expected to arrive the next day, and he was hoping for some quality time with her. But Khan's sleep-busting phone call had cold-showered his plans and Singh wasn't sure what he must do next. He hadn't forgotten the boss's instructions, but decided to call the constables on duty anyway, just to check if everything was okay at the house.

Both men didn't answer and this was bad news. Singh then made the biggest blunder of his life: Disobey Khan.

"No harm in just taking a look-see; I won't enter the house. I need a walk after those cold, tasteless idlis anyway. Why don't these Southie hill dwellers learn to make parathas, for God's sake?"

He did not spot the constable who was meant to guard the entry gate, and there was pin-drop silence. Singh leaned over the wall and saw the blood-drenched bodies of his men lying in a far corner. The policeman in Singh took over, the idlis were forgotten, and so was the command from his superior officer. He placed his hand on his gun, moved to the front door and shouted out:

"Mrs. Khan, are you all right?"

There was no response. He waited for a few moments, brandishing his Colt. Singh called out again, louder this time. All of a sudden, the door creaked open. He entered, his eyes carefully scanning each direction. The trained cop had been through such an event many times before. He was ready to fire, the trigger was half-pressed. The lady of the house was seated on a chair, bound and gagged, her head shaking with fright. As Singh froze, just for a second, Darius, who had climbed up on the window sill located adjacent to the door, pounced on the man. Taken by surprise, and with seventy-five kilograms of flesh and bone falling directly on him, Singh stood little chance. The gun popped out of his hand, as the two men went down sprawling on the wooden floor. Darius grabbed the gun, and pumped three bullets into the policeman's temple.

Zeenat turned her face away in agony. She had thought poorly of Singh from the time she had met him, and even before the door had been opened to let him in, she had feared the worst.

"The portly fool was never going to be a match for this wild beast."

Darius triumphantly sat down on the dead man's chest and stared into his mutilated face, just as a microbiology student would stare into a microscope, trying to figure out a mysterious organism. Blood flowed out from the victim's head just like a machine valve that had developed a major leak.

"What an asshole you are, man, what a fucking asshole. Why would you want to poke your nose into other people's affairs? Now look what you made Uncle Darius do. Tch, tch."

IT WAS LATE IN THE EVENING WHEN KHAN REACHED COONOOR. The cab had been speeding right through, and the only break the driver had been allowed was a quick pee. Khan had thoughtfully bought a pack of chips from the airport, and insisted the driver enjoy them with his foot pressed on the accelerator.

On the way he had tried calling Singh, just to make sure the man hadn't gone out of line, and not getting a response, feared the idiot was already as dead as a dodo. Darius was not a man who would risk keeping a cop a prisoner. He was deeply saddened for the Delhi cop, and more so for his two young children.

Khan accepted this could well be his own last day on the planet, and he had mentally prepared himself for the eventuality. But he needed to ensure no harm came to Zeenat, and for that he would have to think and act smartly with Darius. Any wrong move would immediately endanger his wife's life. Khan had smoked forty cigarettes between Bangalore airport and the bustling Coonoor bus stand. The possibility of death by cancer seemed like a good idea right now. He kept repeating one mantra to himself.

"Engage with the man, Khan, engage with him. Keep talking to him till the right moment for action arrives. *Keep chatting,* don't lose your bloody head."

He asked for the cab to be halted a hundred feet ahead of the bungalow. Khan gave the driver five hundred bucks over and above the agreed fare, and asked him to get out of sight. His booze fund in place, the driver was only too happy to scoot.

He walked to the house slowly in order to avoid unnecessary attention. Khan reached the porch, and ignoring the two dead bodies, knocked softly on the door, which was already ajar.

"Darius, I'm here. Unarmed and alone. Can I come in, please?"

The dreadful laughter, the laughter he detested more than anything in the world.

"Right on boss man, it's your own house!"

DARIUS, SMILING CHEERFULLY, WAS STANDING RIGHT BEHIND his wife. With Singh's Colt pointed to her head. Khan ignored him and looked at Zeenat. Her eyes indicated she was scared, but fine. He was relieved.

"Mister, I am convinced you haven't alerted anyone, and you aren't armed. I don't think you are like that stupid bugger."

Khan turned to look in the direction Darius pointed, and saw Singh's corpse lying in a corner. He sighed.

"Let's end this right now, Darius. Shoot me and be done with it, but let my wife go. She has nothing to do with all this, and you know that."

"Not so fast, inspector, we first need to talk man to man. I want to sort out all the crap my mother has been feeding you. And let me tell you, the reason you find yourself in this mess is that you were so damn confident you could catch me. I saw you spew a lot of arrogant shit on television. And right now, I am thoroughly enjoying the frightened look on your face; it delights my heart. And yes, you've been having many discussions with mad momma, and I want to hear everything."

This was exactly what Khan was hoping for: More time. That alone would possibly save his wife from this crazy bastard.

"Done! Can I sit down?"

"I have a better idea. Let's go to the terrace and chat over booze. Like buddies do. Anyway, I badly need a drink after an entire day of doing nothing. The three idiots were no fun. They died much too soon, and I'm bored. Where do you store the good stuff, officer?"

"It's there in the kitchen cabinet. Should I get it?"

"Yes, please. And do get some ice, and if you have spicy goodies, carry those too and wait for me upstairs. Meanwhile, I shall keep your missus in good spirits. The poor thing will have to sit all alone out here as we men get drunk. Ma'am, would you like to use the toilet again?"

She shook her head, but accepted a sip of water. Zeenat was itching to have a word with Khan, but restrained herself. She knew it was best to keep shut for now, to let her husband figure a way out of the clear and present danger.

THE TWO MEN SAT FACING EACH OTHER ON EASY CHAIRS MADE of cane. Darius started drinking the Scotch on the rocks, while Khan preferred a much diluted version.

"A policeman too scared to drink neat? You disappoint me, man. Maybe it's your way of staying sober tonight, but trust me, you are better off pissed drunk. That's the only way you can get the better of me. Notice that three completely undrunk men are lying lifeless inside your property." Darius plonked his feet on the glass table, making sure they were pointed at Khan's face.

"Darius, why are you doing all this? It's wrong, and it's inhuman. If you have problems, surely there can be a solution. I can try and help you."

His guest laughed out loudly, so loudly it could have been heard at the neighbour's house, located thirty feet away.

"I like you, man, you have balls. And to think you are the one facing some serious problems right now, and only I can try and help you. Problem number one: To try and save your dear wife. Problem number two: To save your own skin. Let's worry about these before you try to unfuck my mind."

"I agree, but surely I can be of help to you in some way. I want to help you, I know where you're coming from."

Darius sat up and refilled his glass. "You don't know shit, because my mom told you the same shit she's been telling everyone else. What did the bitch say? That dad used to beat me up? That he used to beat her up? All bloody lies."

He started rolling a joint. Khan was a bit relieved; this conversation was moving in the right direction. With some weight off his chest, Darius would, hopefully, become a little more reasonable. And that might help in bargaining for Zeenat's life. That's all he wanted to do right now. Find a way to get her out of this place. Once that was achieved, he could try and jump the killer, or trap him in some other way.

"Okay, so you tell me the truth."

"I will, that's why I arranged for this meeting. I'm not going to kill you Khan, don't worry. I want you to be the messenger of truth, and that can't happen if you die. I don't believe in the after-life, else daddy would have returned to fix momma. I don't know if I'll escape alive from here. Maybe you haven't been truthful, maybe a battalion of cops from all over the nation has surrounded this house even as we speak. But it's a chance I am willing to take."

IT WAS MIDNIGHT. KAMBLE HAD CLEARED THE AREA OF COPS, under the pretext of a group briefing at the crime branch office. Khan, wearing a dark hood, something he had never done before, rang Jeroo's doorbell. There was no response for a minute. He rang it again, and then waited. He was aware the arthritic lady would take her time to reach the door.

The door opened slightly, and the woman peered through the gap created by the use of a safety chain. Jeroo employed the chain when visitors disturbed her after nine in the evening, and it was usually the idiotic pizza delivery boy who had read the address incorrectly.

"Who the hell is it?"

"Azeem Khan. Sorry to disturb you at this hour, Mrs. Irani. I have important news of your son."

"Oh god, is he all right?"

"Yes, open the door. I need to speak with you."

The door was yanked open. This was one visitor Jeroo did not mind inviting in as he had always been kind to her. And maybe there was some not very bad news about Darius, though she had prepared herself for the worst.

Khan walked right in and sat himself on the sofa. "Sorry, I'm exhausted. I need a glass of water."

Jeroo was slightly taken aback by this abrupt behaviour from someone she considered to be a gentleman. But right now, all she was interested in was information. "Okay, I shall bring it to you."

As she trotted to the kitchen, Khan quickly removed his shoes, and walked silently behind her. As the lady poured water from a bottle into a stainless steel glass, he covered her mouth and nose with a cloth napkin dipped in chloroform. Old Jeroo turned out to be a tough customer. The struggle lasted all of five minutes, and then she passed out. Khan carried her to the bedroom, and laid her down on the creaking bed.

He placed a pillow on her face, pressed hard, and waited till there was no sign of breathing. "Good riddance, you old bitch. Hope God can find a way to forgive you."

Khan put on his shoes, hooded up, and quietly walked out of the apartment. And hailed a cab. He called Kamble on the way.

"It's done. Thank you."

DARIUS RAN OUT OF ICE.

"Need a refill, sir. Do you mind if I go down and get some rocks? Will you stay put out here like a good boy?"

"I think you are drunk, son. Let me go fetch it."

Darius hollered. "Dude, don't call me 'son', for your own good. I consider it to be a vulgar word. And nope, that much I don't trust you. I am certain you will try to let your sweet lady off. Any half sensible man would do that, and you are an ex bloody cop."

He returned after ten minutes with the bucket reloaded.

"Sorry for the delay, my bladder's gone for a toss in all the excitement. Also had a word with ma'am. She's cool."

Darius poured a large one; Khan was still on his first. He rolled another joint. And then he told his companion his story.

Khan was stunned, but tried his best to stay level-headed. He had to stay focused on the two jobs at hand. One, get Zeenat out of the house. And two, figure a way to over-power this drunk criminal, and get him arrested. He didn't have to worry too long to achieve the second objective.

Without a warning, Darius Irani whipped out Singh's Colt from his pocket and shot himself in the head. The alcohol-filled body crashed to the ground, along with the cane chair. It was all over, just like that. The man Khan had been chasing for weeks had gone without a fuss. And even in death, this chap had scored; he died at the time and place of his choosing, the entire nation's police machinery had failed to get him. Khan spotted a faint smile on the blood-splattered face, a victorious, mocking smile.

After a few moments of mindlessly staring at the corpse, Khan slowly rose to his feet. And kicked the glass table hard, sending the near-empty Teacher's, two glasses, an ice bucket and a plate with a few soggy wafers flying across the terrace.

"Fuck! Fuck! You bastard!" And he climbed down to meet his wife. There was no need to hurry anymore; it was all over.

A FEW WEEKS LATER, KAMBLE TRAVELLED TO COONOOR TO check on Khan. He reached late in the evening and found the man drinking on the porch. He politely declined the offer to join in.

"Sir, I wanted to know if you are all right."

Khan did not reply. Instead, he asked a question related to the media. He had cut all lines of communication with the world below.

"What's the gas on the news channels?"

"They are still singing your praises, sir. There's a lot of hero worship going on and there are petitions to reward you with the Bharat Ratna or something like that."

Khan did not respond, and continued drinking.

"Sir, me and my friends in the forensics department and the hospital where the post-mortem happened took care of things, exactly as you had desired. The closure report says Mrs. Irani had been killed days before her body was found, and that she had been strangled by her mad son, and that his DNA and fingerprints were found on the dead body. As also on the pillow used to strangle her. A couple of CBI officers and a few cops have been suspended on account of negligence, but they will be back in business once the matter cools down. It's all been arranged. Sir, do call me in case you need anything, I shall always be available."

Khan stayed silent. Kamble, realising the objective of his journey had been accomplished, rose to his feet and left. He looked back on his way out and saw Khan mechanically refilling his glass while staring emptily at his apple garden.

AS IT HAD HAPPENED ON MANY OCCASIONS, HIS MIND WENT back to that fateful evening. Khan recalled the serial killer sobbing like a baby as he spoke about sexual abuse; how it had begun when he was only five years old and continued through his school years. And that night when Jeroo Irani put her husband to death by banging the ebony elephant on his head as he slept. The heavy artifact that Rohington Irani had picked up on a trip to Jaipur.

He had returned home unexpectedly that noon, and caught Darius in bed with her. The showdown lasted all day, with the wife sobbing and pleading for mercy, as little Darius sat in a corner, curled up with confusion and fear. She had other plans for the night, but the unsuspecting man had no idea. He had gone to sleep drunk and shattered.

Darius told Khan that Jeroo had bribed the family doctor, Stanley Fernandes, using Ronnie's savings, so that no mention of physical assault was mentioned in the death certificate. And with his help, she had managed to obtain a fake death certificate.

Khan learnt that years of sexual abuse from a young age had turned Darius into an impotent man, a man who had become incapable of normal sexual intercourse. A boy who had grown up to carry extreme hatred against women. Each time he killed, he had felt a great deal of satisfaction, like he had avenged all those years of abuse at the hands of a woman. Darius had considered slaughtering his mother on numerous occasions, but had been unable to bring himself to do it. He had come to enjoy the sight of her living in penury, being mocked by neighbours and other residents.

Yes, all those murders had been liberating, and yes, he had used the same ebony elephant each time. And Darius Irani's final words just before he pulled the trigger:

"Sorry man, on my way up I used the elephant on ma'am. She was a sweet lady, but I couldn't resist it. It had to be done. It was ordained. Please forgive me."